"*Visions of Grace* is an exquisite, perfectly formed little story about big themes: the cruel inevitability of time, the scars formed by past trauma, the aching desire for life—for all our lives—to mean something. It's concise, moving and resonant."

—Gary McMahon, author of the *Concrete Grove* trilogy

"I devoured Alison Littlewood's *Visions of Grace* in almost a single sitting, feverishly turning pages to find out what was going to happen. And then I did. And I still haven't quite recovered. Don't be fooled: Alison Littlewood is a MONSTER. But in the best possible way."

—Daniel Church, author of *The Ravening* and *The Sound of the Dark*

"Mistress of the taut thriller, but always with a magical, mystical undertone."

—Paul Finch, author of *Sacrifice*

Visions of Grace

Visions of Grace

Alison Littlewood

VISIONS OF GRACE
Copyright Alison Littlewood © 2025

Cover Art
Copyright Beatriz Martin Vidal © 2025

Introduction
Copyright Marie O'Regan © 2025

This hardcover edition is published in October 2025 by Absinthe Books, an imprint of PS Publishing Ltd, by arrangement with the author. All rights reserved by the author.

The right of Alison Littlewood to be identified as Author of this Work has been asserted by her in accordance with the Copyright, Designs & Patents Act 1988.

This book is a work of fiction. Names, characters, places and incidents either are products of the author's imagination or are used fictitiously. Any resemblance to actual events or locales or persons, living or dead, is entirely coincidental.

ISBN
978-1-80394-561-3
978-1-80394-560-6 (signed edition)

Design & Layout by Michael Smith
Printed and bound in England by Short Run Press

ABSINTHE BOOKS
PS Publishing | Grosvenor House
1 New Road | Hornsea | HU18 1PG | United Kingdom

editor@pspublishing.co.uk | www.pspublishing.co.uk

Represented by:
Authorised Rep Compliance Ltd.
Ground Floor, 71 Lower Baggot Street
Dublin, D02 P593, Ireland
www.arccompliance.com

Introduction

Alison Littlewood has, by now, firmly established herself as an excellent writer of genre fiction—whether that's supernatural, as with her first novel, *A Cold Season*, *The Unquiet House*, and *Mistletoe*, a true ghost story for Christmas, or thrillers, such as *Path of Needles*. In addition, Alison often incorporates aspects of folklore or fairy tale into her writing to great effect (notable examples include her later novels under the pen-name A.J. Elwood, *The Cottingley Cuckoo* and *The Other Lives of Miss Emily White*). It's been my pleasure over the years to include her in a number of anthologies I've edited, either alone or with my husband, Paul Kane; she never disappoints, and with this novella, Alison has proved that once again.

Visions of Grace is a tale of what it means to be a parent, and of the profound impact a mother—or the lack of one during our formative years—has on a child; an effect that reverberates forward into adulthood, hiding—burying—itself deep into the psyche. The story's protagonist, the eponymous Grace, is alone in the world—the loss of her mother at a young age merely the first in a series of losses that have left her adrift. She's formed a friendship with her next-door neighbour, Leanne, and become fond of her children—especially six-year-old Katie, who's excited for her birthday party. In the run up to this, Grace starts having visions of something disastrous happening—can she stop it? Can she save Katie, even herself? Emotional, unsettling… *Visions of Grace* will pull you inexorably along until it reaches its shattering conclusion.

Turn the page and find out how.

—Marie O'Regan
Derbyshire, April 2025

Visions of Grace

*For Marie and Paul.
Thank you for everything you do
for this genre of ours.*

PROLOGUE
When I was Five

The earliest memory I possess is of my mother's face. I was lying in bed, clutching my cuddly bunny, and I was five-and-a-half years old plus a couple of weeks. That part of it is something I know, rather than something I remember. There isn't that much to this memory at all, and yet it's the most precious one I have.

My bedroom door was ajar and the hall light was on. That door made a noise when it was opened, kind of hissing over the pile of the carpet, and that's what came first, that sound. The light grew brighter, yellow and warm, making me blink. Then it darkened again as my mother stood in front of it and pulled the door to behind her. There was a pause, and it seemed to me so long; surely too long. Mum didn't normally wait like that, she always said she was too busy to stand about doing nothing. She'd just say, "Time to sleep, Gracie," and walk right in.

Her stillness was starting to make me feel a bit funny, but then she moved, and it was just Mum, coming like she always did to tuck me in. That night was different in another way too, though, because she still hadn't said anything. She leaned over me and at first her face was in shadow, then she tilted her head, and I saw her as clearly as if she were caught in a photograph; so that, long afterward, I would wonder if that was all this was, a confusion of memory with some picture I'd once seen.

It couldn't have been, though, because Mum never looked like that in any of her photos.

In photos, Mum was always smiling.

That night, she didn't smile. She stayed as she was, looking down at me, and she still didn't speak, and she didn't tuck me in. I looked back at her and saw all of the things that were in her eyes or perhaps the things that weren't and I remember parting my lips—I can still hear the little sound they made—to say something to her, to make her move, to be my mum again, but I couldn't think of the right words and so instead I started to cry.

Later, I never could be quite sure if it was something that really happened or if it was just in my head. Years went by, as years do. Memories get jumbled by time and new experiences and our own shortcomings, everything mingling and blurring, given shape only by our effort to recollect, to hold onto what has long since slipped away. I'm no different to anyone else in that regard. Still, her face as she leaned over me remains as vivid as if she were still alive. It's difficult to summon an image of her wearing any other expression. It's as if I'm stuck in that moment: Mum standing there, staring down at me, as if seeing everything—my future, or perhaps her own. Seeing all that I had inside, everything I *was*. Taking those things into herself and not smiling.

That was Mum's last night on earth. The next day, she was gone. An absence, yet so very much there. She was present in the way I would get myself dressed for school, picking out my own clothes. She was there in the way I got my own breakfast, ignoring the stink of stale beer that drifted from the empty bottles piled next to the bin. She was there in Dad's eyes, in the way he didn't laugh any longer, in the way he sometimes forgot to give me a hug when I walked out of the door. And in the way he sometimes hugged me too tight, his breath thick with that same sour smell, and I would feel the tears leaking down his cheeks, the wet, scratchy stubble on his chin.

I don't remember anything else from when I was five-and-a-half. I only know that Mum was there and then she wasn't. There's nothing else until I was seven, eight, nine. Just that: a single look, and she was gone.

CHAPTER ONE

Five Days to the Party

"Of course, she married the prince. She lived happily ever after." I smile down at Katie—dark hair, pink cheeks, eyes shining a little too brightly with the excitement of a visitor and possibly too much sugar. Katie is almost six years old. She's bright and beautiful and alive, and I'm not sure she's going to sleep for a while yet, but I kiss her forehead and switch off her lamp. When I reach the doorway, turning to watch her shuffle deeper under her quilt, I have a sudden image of what I must look like; a dark silhouette against the light coming from the hall, just standing there. I shake away the shadow of a memory that doesn't belong in this place or this moment. This isn't one last glimpse, doesn't have any particular meaning; it's nothing like that. I'm not even Katie's mum.

"Are you coming for my birthday, Auntie Grace?" Katie's voice banishes the thought, and I'm glad to let it go.

"I am, sweetheart. I'm going to help out with your friends. And games. And cake."

"Goody." Despite her excitement, she sounds half-asleep. "Daisy is coming. And Isla. And Ruby and Em. And JoJo. She's my very best friend."

I tell her that I know she is. She's told me this already, many times, though it still makes me smile. She plays with JoJo a lot. She and Katie are so alike, they could almost be sisters. They're similar in other ways, too.

Partners in crime, her mum Leanne always says, and they are; co-conspirators. I can almost hear a peal of their matching giggles, see their matching white grins, their hair done up in matching pigtails, likely with matching pink bobbles, too.

I turn to go just as Katie says, "I love you, Auntie Grace."

My breath catches in my throat and it takes a moment for me to reply. When I manage "You too, sweetie," my voice is a little hoarse. I add "Night night," pull her door to and leave her to dreamland.

Leanne is downstairs, a glass of white wine clutched in her hand, another on the coffee table waiting for me. "Thank God," she mouths at me. "I adore her, but sometimes..." She grins as if to say, *You know the end of that sentence*.

And I do. I'm not a real aunt. I moved next door to Leanne when Katie was two, and like any kid, she's always been non-stop, a whirl, a flurry. Tonight, I only popped round for a couple of hours, but still I feel like I could go on sinking down and down into the sofa, until there's nothing around me but cushions and the welcome dark.

But as I clink glasses with Leanne, I also know that the end of her sentence would have been a lie. She'd do anything for her kids. She's a great mum, a brilliant mum. I don't suppose I'm best placed to know that, really, but I still do. It doesn't matter how tired she is; Leanne is always ready to make sure Katie eats properly, to answer her endless questions, to do her hair yet again, to comfort her if she cries.

Most important of all: she's *there*.

The wine seeps into me, cool and crisp, but it spreads warmth through me anyway. I smile at the thought of Katie upstairs, drifting off with that *happily ever after* in her head.

Occasionally, the mood would take my dad to tell me stories, but they were never quite right. Mainly they were about me: pretty, magical, yet unfinished tales about where I came from, about how a stork came and dropped me down the chimney, or how he found me under a gooseberry bush, or made me out of snow and I came to life. Or about how I'd been abandoned in the forest, like Gretel, only Dad rescued me and brought me home to our little house just outside Leeds. It wasn't until much later that I realised: he always told me stories with no mums in them. At best, there were wicked stepmothers who didn't want little girls. Mostly though, they were about children who had simply burst into being, aged a day or a year or five-and-a-half, ready-made and whole. His stories didn't really go anywhere. They had no *what happened next*. There were no real endings, only beginnings, and that was all right; I never did press him to go on, not like Katie. I was happy just to stay there. I wanted to remain nestled in those moments he created for us, a little girl and her dad and a place where they could be whole.

He never told me the full story, not really, and that wasn't altogether his fault. I felt like we were skirting a land that was vast and dark and empty, a black void I was afraid to fall into.

Here, in Leanne's little home, I can tell new stories, proper ones, with magic at their heart. I can sense it all around me, that magic; in the simple happiness of a child, in the thing that is shared by those who live under this roof.

I love you, Auntie Grace.

I open my mouth to tell Leanne I've been proclaimed an honorary relative, ready to adopt a light-hearted tone even though the import of it is swelling inside me, when the front door—which lets straight into the lounge—rattles open and two girls burst in. It's Leanne's elder daughter, Chloe, and her friend, Shannon, both seventeen, all skinny arms and white grins and long, gleaming hair, and suddenly the room is full of noise. Chloe's just passed her driving test, though Shannon failed her first one and insists that all the best drivers pass on their second, and anyway Chloe will just have to drive her around in Leanne's Corsa, unless of course she's too busy with her *boooyfrieeeend*...

"Oh my God, *as if*. Shan, you are so *extra*." Chloe squeals with laughter and pushes her friend away, and as soon as they pause for breath, I congratulate her and tell them I'll leave them in peace.

When I've said my goodbyes and am standing outside in the quiet, it's rather a case of the opposite; like I've stepped out into peacefulness, leaving the chaos inside. I can still hear their chatter, muted by the closed door, and I pause for a minute and look up at the sky. The season is sliding deeper into autumn and there's a cold nip and an early dark. It's never truly dark, here, though; the clouds reflect back the ambient light that rises from the houses all around me, and I can't see a single star. I don't really mind that. Vicky Ave, as we term Victoria Avenue, isn't that different from where I grew up; this part of Leeds is all rows of terraces, one after the next, differing only in the age of the paint around the window frames, the shape of the cracks in the paving of their front yards, the tone and brilliance of the light shining through the curtains.

It isn't altogether quiet, either. Behind me I can still hear the sounds of life, of a *family*, and from somewhere else, Rihanna compares her love to the stars in the sky. My own place however, just next door, is silent, and its windows are dark. I close my eyes for a moment and breathe, as if I'm sharing in it just a little while longer, before returning to my empty home. I hadn't always thought it would be that way—I'd had a boyfriend when I bought the place, Connor, and things had been said about him moving in. There had been visions of a house with lights on and enfolding arms waiting when I walked in, and one day, I'd imagined, kids with my hair and his eyes...

I shake that thought away. I tell myself I'm happy with what I have.

I love you, Auntie Grace.

I don't even need my own lights on, with so many others around me. The Farleys' motion-sensor spotlight, opposite, is so bright it practically lights up the whole street. Right on cue, it flicks on: *Thank you, Farleys.* I close Leanne's gate behind me and step onto the pavement and hear another sound: the cooling engine of Leanne's Corsa, still ticking softly to itself. It's all on-street parking around here and the cars are nose-to-tail all the way down one side of the road, narrowing the carriageway. I can't even see my own little Toyota, but Chloe's been lucky; she's snagged a spot right outside. A tight one, too, though she's managed to park dead-on straight to the kerb: *Well done, Chloe.*

I walk the short distance to my own gate and go up the path to my front door. I pull the keys from my jeans pocket and, though I'm standing between the door and the Farleys' light, casting everything into deep shadow, I select the right key and slide it into the lock without hesitation. Why not? This is my place, I know exactly where everything is, and I walk into my lounge and flick the switch without looking. Light floods the room and I almost cry out.

A little girl is sitting on my sofa. Katie is sitting on my sofa. I can't think how she got here, though in an instant, in my mind, I have pictured her getting out of bed, walking downstairs—*on her own*—through Leanne's lounge—*still on her own*—and slipping out of the door—*past us, she'd have had to go* past *us, without our seeing*—and then somehow beating me down the street—*and letting herself in*—to my house.

I love you, Auntie Grace.

It's like something out of a fairy tale, all the ones my dad never finished, children springing into existence simply for the wishing, so that I don't know *how*, can't think of the trick of it. Katie goes on looking at me and I look back. I don't speak and neither does she. Then I blink and suddenly realise it isn't Katie at all. It's JoJo, her friend, her very best friend. Her hair isn't up in pigtails now, though, isn't neatly tied with bobbles. Her dark locks are hanging draggled in front of her eyes and she's peering through them, staring straight at me, and she doesn't blink and her face is so still—

My heart stutters. When I draw breath I hear a dry rattle; my lungs feel tight, like scrunched-up paper bags. I can't think how JoJo came to be here. I suppose she must have come to play with Katie, but they'd never mentioned it next door. Or perhaps she never made it there? Maybe she somehow got the wrong house. I must have left the kitchen door open and she came in via the back lane. That wouldn't have been like me, not at all, or like her, but it must be so—mustn't it?

I find I still haven't spoken. I'm still staring at her, like she's a ghost. How long has she been sitting there, swinging her legs, the heels of her Mary Janes tapping my sofa? How long was she sitting in the *dark*?

"JoJo," I manage. My voice is hoarse, for entirely different reasons than when I said goodnight to Katie. "What are you doing in here, sweetheart? Are you all right?"

JoJo doesn't answer. She just goes on looking at me, then—as if there's nothing weird about any of this—she pushes herself to her feet. She's all dressed up. She's wearing a flared pink dress and patterned white tights. She twirls a little one way, then the other, as if showing me the way the skirt swings around her legs. She smiles at me.

"What a pretty frock," I say. "You look ready for the party, JoJo! Look, let's get you home, shall we?"

Even as I say the words, I realise I don't know where she lives. I'm not one of the mums, after all; I'm not in that crowd. I don't stand with them at the school gates, sharing gossip and phone numbers and arranging visits and sleepovers for the kids at this house or that. Still, I pull my mobile from my back pocket and give JoJo a look that's meant to be reassuring as I scroll to Leanne's number. She answers almost at once. I can hear Chloe and Shannon, still teasing and laughing in the background.

"Grace, hey!" she says. "Everything all right? Did you forget something?"

I try to explain, though I can't, not really. "No—Lee, it's JoJo. She's here. I suppose she must have been looking for Katie, and—no, I know. I don't know."

As I talk, JoJo starts to prance up and down my lounge. She skips a few steps, twirls about, skips back again. "I don't know what to do, if I'm honest. I don't even know her family. Can I bring her to you, and you could call them? Okay? Great."

JoJo's pacing has carried her just behind me. I turn, pasting a bright smile onto my face, preparing to tell her she's going to Katie's—and JoJo isn't there.

I raise my gaze to the kitchen door. She must have kept right on going, into the next room; the door is ajar, but there's no light on in there. I follow in her footsteps, reach out and flick it on. Light spills across the counter tops, cupboard doors, the fridge, the bin, a couple of stools. Still no JoJo.

It's a small room. There's nowhere to hide. It's as if she's vanished into the air.

I look at the back door, which is next to the fridge. It must be unlocked, because how else had she got in?

I feel like I'm telling myself fairy stories.

I go to check, even though part of me is insisting, in a quiet voice, that I would have heard it open if JoJo had just gone out. My back door rattles. It sticks. I keep meaning to take a file to the edge of the wood, something else I haven't got round to, though *Connor would have, if Connor were here*. I shake that thought away. I simply haven't, which means that door would have been loud as it opened and loud as it closed again behind her and, what's more, my back garden has a floodlight which, like the Farleys', is motion-sensitive. It would have lit up like day the second she stepped outside, but there's a glass panel in the door and it's so dark out there I can't even see the lawn or the shrubbery or the shed. That pane of glass is like a mirror, and in it is nothing but a reflection of my own pale face.

I stare into my eyes. I stare just as JoJo had, sitting on my sofa, through straggles of her untidy, straggly hair.

I go to the back door anyway. I reach out and press down on the handle. It moves just a little, then stops. I try again, but it doesn't yield. My back door is locked. Of course it is; it always was. I never go out and leave my house unlocked…

I let out an odd sound, one I'm glad no one else can hear.

I picture JoJo, pacing up and down my lounge. Perhaps I'd lost track of where she was; yes, that must have been it. She'd actually skipped across to the other side of the room, where the stairs are.

Ignoring the fresh protests from the back of my mind—*I would have seen her*—I go back into the lounge, stand at the foot of the steps set into one side of the room, and call out, "JoJo?"

My voice sounds almost afraid. How silly, to be afraid: she's only a child.

Perhaps it's just that I'm not used to them, that's all, not being a mum. If I *was* a mum, this would all seem fine. I wouldn't be feeling the pricklings of fear on the back of my neck...

It comes to me then that they are playing a trick. Katie and JoJo, JoJo and Katie: *co-conspirators*. *Thick as thieves*. Perhaps Leanne's a part of this too, and Chloe and Shannon. Maybe they think it's hilarious. It's easy to picture a couple of teenagers collapsing against each other and laughing fit to bust. Perhaps Katie, as she lay in bed, as she told me she loved me, was trying her very hardest not to giggle. I try to think how they must have done it. Did they manage to pinch my keys, let JoJo in, leaving her here alone before they somehow replaced them? And then what? Did they also locate the back door key I keep out of sight on the edge of a shelf in a high cupboard, have her sneak out—and lock up again after herself?

Maybe she'd sprayed the hinges with WD40 while she was at it.

I shake my head, returning to the present. I'm standing at the top of the stairs, staring at closed doors. Quickly, I look into my bedroom, then the spare and the box room—the one that, in Leanne's house, is Katie's, though I keep it as a study. Finally, I check the bathroom. I pull back the shower curtain and look inside the bath. Then I try the bedrooms again, yanking open wardrobe doors, peering under beds. I already know she isn't here. She isn't anywhere.

A ghost. The word wanders through my mind and I banish it. JoJo is fine. *Fine*.

It comes to me that, next door, Leanne is waiting for me. She must be wondering where the hell I am.

Maybe that's where JoJo has gone. She got past me somehow. She'd got the wrong house, that was all, and now she's found the right one.

Or perhaps the trick they're playing, this really clever, though rather mean trick, is over. JoJo will be sitting where she should be, on Leanne's sofa and not mine. She'll be squeezed in between Chloe and Shannon, and Katie will have jumped out of bed and they'll all be waiting for me, laughing and wondering what took me so long.

Visions of Grace

I walk back down the stairs, through the lounge and out of my front door. I close it behind me, on my house, my *empty* house. My hand goes to my pocket, automatically checking my keys are there, and I hurry down the drive and along the pavement and back to Leanne's. Her door opens before I reach it. She is already waiting for me, a mum, someone who knows everything about what kids are like and what they get up to and what ought to be done, and she calls out, "Grace, where's JoJo? You haven't *left* her—"

On her own, that's the end of her sentence, though I don't need to hear it. I can make out everything I need to from her tone, the concern in her voice.

"She's not with you?" I stop dead, glance over my shoulder. "Lee—I think she's gone. I lost sight of her, for a *second*, and she—"

Leanne glances back into her own lounge before stepping out. "It's okay. We'll fetch her. Katie's fine, Chloe can keep an eye on her, if she wakes up."

Leanne would never leave a small child alone, not for a second, that's what she's showing me. Not like I must have. I want to tell her I *haven't*, I *didn't*, but my throat is closing up.

"Come on." Leanne takes my arm, gives me a smile. She doesn't look mean, doesn't look like she's playing any kind of game. She's being as she is, all mum, all soothing and reassurance as she steers me back towards my home. I unlock the door, fumbling a little with the key this time, and we step into the empty lounge.

"She was right there." I point towards the place on the sofa, as if that will make JoJo appear again, legs a-swinging, tappety-tap. Of course, she doesn't.

"Tell me from the beginning," Leanne says. "What happened?"

So I do, and as I form the words Leanne's frown grows deeper, cutting grooves into her face. "All right. I don't like this." She takes her mobile from her pocket. "I'm calling her mum." She taps the screen, presses the phone to her ear. It's like she's trying to shut me out, though I can still faintly hear a woman's voice as the call is answered.

"Holly? It's Leanne. Sorry to bother you, only a friend of ours saw JoJo, just a couple of minutes ago, actually, but she seems to have run off and hidden or something, and we wondered if you were about."

The reply is rapid and I can't make out the words but the tone is tinged with surprise. Leanne casts a glance at me then turns a little away, so I can't see her expression. "Really? She is? Are you *sure*, Holl, because—"

That voice again, insistent, and Leanne says, "Of course, I'll hold on."

She twists back towards me for a moment, like JoJo in her party dress, a little twirl this way and back again, and words bubble once more from the phone and Leanne holds it horizontally between us, so that I can hear this new voice.

"—*sleeping*, Mummy. You didn't have to tuck me in *again*—"

It's JoJo. She sounds tired and cross but even so I can tell that it's her, and then Holly is back, saying, "Yep, definitely here! In bed—woken up now, though, probably won't settle again for ages, but yes, she's safe and sound."

Leanne holds out the accusing rectangle of light for a moment longer, then puts the phone back to her ear. She apologises and says her goodbyes and ends the call. As she speaks, I'm waiting for her to turn to me. To look at me with a new expression in her eyes. I'm waiting for her to demand an explanation, to unravel what I can't, because it doesn't make any sense. None of this can actually have happened, and I can't make it okay because it obviously *isn't*.

Maybe she's about to ask what the fuck is wrong with me.

My head is suddenly throbbing. I had been so happy when Katie said *I love you, Auntie Grace*. I'd stood and looked at her and drunk in those words and for a moment, just a *moment*, I had felt that thing that lived under Leanne's roof, settling down upon my shoulders. Perhaps that's what this was really about. Perhaps it was feeling that way, seeing them that way, Katie and Leanne and Chloe, together, so happy, all the beautiful chaos that meant *family*. Perhaps I had missed that more than I could ever allow myself to realise or to say, and then I'd come back here, to my peaceful but quiet, empty house, and—

What?

My gaze goes to the mirror over the fireplace. I can't see anything reflected in it from this angle except the light fitting, but I point to it and say, "God, Leanne, I'm so sorry. I must just have—I mean, it was dark. I came in and maybe I was a bit spooked, all the lights were off, and I wonder if I saw my own bloody reflection? Only Katie was so sweet, I was still thinking of her, and JoJo looks so very like her. I must have thought—"

My voice tails away. Of course it does. It makes no sense whatsoever. Though, I realise, perhaps it actually *does*. Perhaps it was exactly the way I'd described, my mind supplying what I'd wanted to see, what I'd been thinking of. But the rational part of me had known it couldn't be so, I'd just left Katie behind me, in bed for God's sake, so my imagination had filled in the gap with JoJo instead.

That skirt, twirling. Feet, tapping. The way she'd stared, straight ahead, through her draggled hair...

"I'm so sorry," I say again, and a new thought comes to me, whole and hopeful. "The wine, you know? It must have gone to my head. I have been pretty tired lately."

Leanne gives a wry smile and lets out a spurt of air, not quite a laugh. "Well, I know how that goes."

Of course you do, I think. *You're always tired. But you don't see imaginary children sitting on your sofa...*

Still, Leanne's smile warms a little as we say goodnight once more. "Right, are you safe to leave on your own? No getting spooked this time," she jokes, and I force myself to laugh, though it sounds dry and a little weird, like it didn't come from me at all.

When she's gone, I close the door and lean back against it. From here I can see the whole of the lounge, the stairs leading upward and the open door into the kitchen, all the lights on now. I decide I'll make some tea. I'll make tea because that's normal, and it will make me feel more normal, too.

I go in, grab a mug and set the kettle boiling. While I wait, I stand in front of the back door and stare into the glass. I still can't see outside. *Stupid*, I whisper, and clench my hands into fists. In the window, my face is pale and unformed and blank, as if it's waiting to see what shape the world will assume before it decides what expression to adopt.

I remain motionless and listen for the kettle switching itself off, and it does, but still I go on staring. I stand there for what seems a very long time, and all I see is me.

Chapter Two
Four Days to the Party

The next day, I get to the office early. I make coffee for one, since the rest of the accounts team won't be in for half an hour, and start processing invoices from the suppliers of wood, stone and brick we use in our construction projects. I have to force myself to concentrate, but I'm glad I'm here, not at home. Every time I pause and close my eyes I keep seeing her there: JoJo, sitting on my sofa in that little pink dress, her party dress. Perhaps that's why my mind keeps skipping forward as well as back. I keep seeing a party—Katie's party—with a whole bunch of little girls, and of course her very best friend. I made my promise to help out ages ago, though now I find myself wondering if I should go back on it. I don't altogether want to see JoJo again. I'm not sure that being with her in real life will banish the image stuck in my head: JoJo with a strange, fixed expression on her face, her hair hanging down in front of her eyes.

I can only hope that it will. I've been friends with Leanne for a long time. I don't want to let her down and I'm already mortified about what she must think. Cancelling would only strain our relationship further. And I *like* living next door to her. I'm on my own—Dad died three years ago, and a lot of my old schoolmates have moved away. Connor is long gone, of course, and no one else is on the horizon. Leanne's alone, too, apart from the girls. Chloe's dad died when she was a toddler and Katie's isn't in their life. That's what Leanne told me, like he was a mistake she wanted to forget, and I was happy to help her do that. She's always been there and so have I—someone to laugh with, cry with, share a bottle of wine with.

What must she think of me now?

Whatever that is, I need to cover it over. I need to be me again, solid, reliable Grace. Of course I'm going to help her with the party.

I return to the invoices, find one for clay pantiles that hasn't been signed off by the project manager, no delivery note to be found. I put it in query and take a sip of coffee, which is already going cold. My eyes slip out of focus and for a moment, I imagine JoJo sitting in the chair at the desk opposite mine. All dressed up in her party frock, but in the wrong place, the wrong time. I shake the image away. Do I really have such a gaping hole in my life—one where a child should be? Or is this all born of another kind of wish, the thought of a little girl and her mum—did I miss that so badly growing up that I've started seeing things? I'm not some nut job. It's not as if I'd ever want to snatch JoJo and steal her away. What would I even do with her? Anyway, I *like* my peace and quiet. A party, a whole bunch of little girls, will probably drive me to distraction. I'm *glad* none of those kids will be going anywhere near my world, my place, my life. I'm going to be in theirs for a just little while, that's all, before I return—gratefully—to normality.

I hear a tired murmur of *Morning* and look up to see everyone arriving at once: Sue, an older lady who handles our payroll; the finance director, Neil, right behind her, slipping off his jacket; behind him, Jude, the new girl in marketing; and someone else I can't quite see. Probably Emily, her colleague. I push myself up, offering to make fresh coffee all round. Sue says "Bless you," and Neil says "Thanks, love." Jude gives me a wave and keeps on going towards a bank of desks at the other end of the office, and I see who was standing behind her.

It's Chloe.

I half-expect her to walk off down the aisle after Jude, resolving into

Visions of Grace

Emily after all, but she doesn't. She doesn't move. She stands and stares right at me and I feel the wrongness of it in my bones.

I try to tell myself it shouldn't feel *off* that she's here. She's my friend's— my very *best* friend's—daughter. We've never really had any connection other than through Leanne, but maybe she's decided she wants to see me for some reason of her own. Maybe she wants to plan some surprise for her mum. And she's just passed her driving test. Maybe she fancied a run out and was passing and thought she'd bob in and say hello. She shouldn't have been able to walk right in but Stef, our receptionist, is probably late, and someone might have held the office door open for her, not realising it was a stranger walking in behind them.

Chloe is wearing a ruffled top in soft baby pink. It's not like anything I've seen her in before. The colour is Katie's favourite, not Chloe's. Why would she wear it now?

My mind is babbling. Chloe is staring and my mind is babbling, and I know I'm trying to make this feel ordinary when something inside me knows it's *not*.

Still, I go on reaching. Maybe Chloe heard about my odd episode last night. She must have; Leanne would have told her. Maybe she thinks I'm mad. She wants to warn me off her family, away from her mum, away from Katie.

Chloe's mouth falls open. Just like that her jaw drops, as if she's seen something terrible, her eyes fixed on me, she still hasn't looked away, and it comes to me that she is screaming. There's no sound I can hear, none at all, but I almost *do* hear it, going on and on...

A hand drops onto my shoulder and I snap my head around to see Sue's face up close to mine. She's wearing a concerned expression and I wonder what I must look like. Pale? Shocked? My eyes feel so wide they might be pinned open. I make a smothered sound and her frown deepens. Her mouth makes an odd, repetitive movement, then sound comes back to me and I realise she's saying my name, over and over. It doesn't quite seem to mean anything, though, or perhaps it means something else, something different than it used to. A question, not a certainty. *Grace... Grace... Grace...?*

I look past her, back to where my friend's child had been standing, but Chloe is gone. There's only an empty space where she had been and behind that, Alex from sales, just arriving, dropping a jumper over the back of his chair.

"Grace, Are you all right?"

I try to tell Sue that of course I am. I was just having a moment, I'm fine, but even as I say the words, I'm shaking her off. Just a moment, that's all, I *need some air*, though that's not what I'm after. I stride past Alex towards the door. I weave around another bunch of people on their way into reception—Stef is here after all, coat off, headset on, all settled—and burst out of the big glass doors at the front of the building, into the car park.

I scan the cars, looking for Leanne's Corsa. I can't see it anywhere. Surely I would? It's bright red, and Chloe can't have walked back out here, got into the car, started it up and vanished around the corner so fast. There's only a narrow exit and it's a busy time, lots of people driving in, parking up, blocking the way. She'd have had to go slow, not that she'd be rushing, she'd be checking her seatbelt and mirror, she's practically still a learner.

If she were ever here.

If I'm not going mad.

I look up once more and catch the eye of Frank, one of the purchasing team. He's just going inside, giving me an odd look. I try a smile, though it feels more like a grimace on my face and he quickly looks away. Sue catches up with me, pushing a glass of water into my hands. Why does she have a glass of water in the car park? She gives me a little nod, as if it's the usual thing, and I take it from her and sip. I smile at her, more to make her feel better than anything else. I just want her to stop looking at me that way.

I take a deep breath of cool morning air. The water does help, a little. I apologise to Sue, tell her again that I was only having a moment. I *was*, though now I've got my glass of water and some fresh air and Chloe is gone, and I'm *fine*. Everything is totally, completely ordinary.

Sue still hovers at my shoulder and so I attempt a joke. "Sorry I'm late with the coffee," and her smile becomes real as she pats my back. She's accepting my words, allowing this to slide into the past, happy to have everything smoothed over and explained away, whatever this was.

What *was* it? Was Chloe ever even here?

And if she wasn't, where is she now?

Most importantly—was she *screaming?*

It comes to me that I should ring Leanne. That's what she'd do, isn't it? Chloe is my best friend's daughter and I want to know where she is. But it comes to me that I can't. Last night, and now this? I *can't*. Nope. I'm not going to give way before some weird turn and make everything worse. Not. Going. To. Happen.

Even Sue looks happier now, and if Sue can accept that everything is fine, well, it must be. Sue is the epitome of normal. She acts like she's everybody's mum. She has a husband called Mark and they go to Tenerife on their holidays every year and have a daughter who's in teacher training and a fat little dachshund called Rolo. Now she puts out a hand and relieves me of the glass, though I could have carried it back in by myself. She's wearing her favourite cardie, one she knitted herself. I feel the fluffy peach wool brushing against my arm and try to feel the ordinariness bleeding from her and seeping into me.

I glance around the car park. A car park Chloe could never have vanished from so quickly.

At least I didn't tell anyone that she was here. She *wasn't* here. She couldn't have been here, could she? Just like JoJo was never there, and JoJo was *fine*. She was at home in bed all along.

The only one not fine was me.

Well, now I am. That's all there is to it.

Sue and I turn to go inside. As we head towards the door, which is made of glass tinted in mirrored bronze, I see the reflection of clouds, and something else; something moving where nothing should be.

I whirl—*twirl*—around in time to see what had been reflected there. There's a balloon, drifting into the colourless sky. It's a metallic baby pink. There is writing on it. It's in the shape of a heart and it catches the light for a moment, sending back a glint like a sharp smile as it floats higher.

Back at my desk once more, I sip at my coffee—which Neil went and made, in my absence—and bow my head over my work. I can't focus on any of it and eventually, I give in. I pull my phone from my bag. I'm not going to ring Leanne, of course not, but I can drop her a text, can't I? As a friend. Her very best friend.

I shake my head—*I'm not six*—and tap on the screen.

Hey, just checking in! Sorry I had a weird moment last night. Don't trust me with wine! :-D I didn't properly congratulate Chloe. Tell her well done from me. What's she up to?

I stare at the screen. Delete the last sentence. Replace it with:

Bet she's zooming about all over the place!

I switch the exclamation for a question mark, add a couple of kisses, and before I can change my mind, hit SEND. The message turns blue; too late now. Still, I read it over and over again, wondering if I worded it right. A second later, the answer lands on my screen.

Don't worry! Weirdo ;-) Will do but it'll have to wait cos she's still in bed!!! I've been up hours!! Katie all excited like she thinks it's her birthday already. Wuz a relief to drop her at school! Kids!!! :-D

Well, that clears that one up.

Visions of Grace

Chloe's safe, she's in bed, just as JoJo was, she's not here or anywhere, and she certainly isn't screaming. She isn't staring like that and she isn't wearing some ruffly pink top, something she'd never choose.
Unless she was wearing it for Katie.
I'm clearly going out of my mind.
Another second and a new message lands on my screen.

Come round? Tomorrow night? We'll talk party. I'll risk that wine :-D

I sit back in my chair and close my eyes and see again that heart-shaped bubble of metallic pink floating up, up, into the dull, flat sky. I see again that flash of light, like a grin, there and then gone. And I see the words emblazoned in a cheery font across the middle of the balloon.
Happy Birthday!
And beneath them, a big, unmistakeable number *6*.

Chapter Three
Three Days to the Party

When the following evening comes, Leanne greets me at the door and hands me a glass of wine before I can even step inside, as if there's no question of worrying about the other night any longer, and the weight that's settled around my shoulders lifts a little. It has lain heavy upon me; I got through work like an automaton—thankfully no visions, not today—but still, I couldn't get Leanne and Katie and Chloe out of my mind. I couldn't stop wondering, *Why couldn't she have seen me last night? Doesn't she sense the urgency?* And, like pins pressing into my skin: *Didn't she* want *to see me?*

But of course, there is no sense of urgency about Leanne. Why should there be? I try to damp down my own, just as I hear Chloe's voice from somewhere behind her. My heart contracts, but when her face appears over Leanne's shoulder and she looks so much herself, so blithe, so confident, *happy*—not screaming, so very far from screaming—I just feel relieved.

"Cheers," I say, and take the tiniest sip, because it had to be the wine, I'd had too much or maybe it was off, and when I went into work the next morning I must have been a little bit hung over, and it had put weird images in my head. There's no way that's happening again. It *hasn't*.

Visions of Grace

"Come on then," Leanne says. "Plan of attack," though I hardly hear her words through the *Auntie Grace!* that's bellowed out of the door.

Katie appears, her dark hair pulled back in a pony tail. "I love you!"

I laugh; we all do. And my heart warms, and I take another sip, and we sit together around the coffee table, which has a list of party games and another of food as well as a whole scribbly mass of Katie's drawings. There are stick figures holding hands with spidery fingers: short ones, tall ones, middling ones, ones with yellow hair or brown or black, all wearing triangular skirts in bright colours, though the red of their grins is all the same.

And everything is all right. It *is*. I keep blocking out the image of Chloe that tries to fill my mind. Of JoJo, sitting on the sofa between us. They don't belong here, not now, not even in my head. There's absolutely no reason that everything isn't okay, and there's nothing wrong with me. Did I really think I was losing it—why? Because I didn't have a mum growing up? That's just the way it was. It happens. It's not like it messed me up. *Look at me*, I keep thinking, as if to reassure myself. *Sitting here, with a family, and I'm not jealous, not bitter, I'm not some sad, lonely person stuck on the outside. I'm here. Katie loves me, and I love her too, and Leanne, and Chloe, because they're my friends.*

I glance around at all their faces, loving them and feeling happy to be a part of this, planning a birthday party, what could be better than that? And sipping my wine, which has gone down quicker than I'd intended, though Leanne tops it up and gives me a wink. Hers is still full. I take another sip to show my appreciation, though what I'm really drinking down is the atmosphere, this thing they have between them, this beautiful thing, and that is the sweetest taste of all.

We talk about pass the parcel and musical chairs and grandmother's footsteps for a bit, Katie insisting, "I want to play tig!" and making us laugh again. Then we move on to food and she demands jelly and ice cream, and she jumps in again with something about a clown; Ruby had a clown at her party, she says, and Leanne reminds her that she hated the clown, she was scared of the clown and cried and had to go home, and Leanne has already asked her if she wanted one this time and Katie had said no. Her daughter closes her lips with a little snap, not looking very happy, and Leanne changes the subject. She gets her to recite the names of her friends who are coming, and Katie does.

"Daisy and Ruby and Em," she says. "And Isla. And Chloe and Shannon."

"Who else?" Leanne says. "That's not all, is it?"

I shift in my seat, waiting for her to say the name, but she doesn't. Instead she says, "Chloe's boyfriend," and giggles.

"Oh—em—gee," Chloe proclaims, giving Katie a mock push. "That is *so* cringe. You've been listening to Shan. He is not—like, no way. Anyway, he's not invited."

Katie's rich giggle rises into the air and Leanne, as tactful as ever, interrupts. "Well, who else?"

Her daughter chants. "JoJoJoJoJo!"

"Of *course* JoJoJoJoJo," Leanne replies, and I try not to picture JoJo but in spite of myself it feels like she's been there all along, sitting between us, drumming her feet on the sofa, all dressed up in her little pink party dress and staring through straggly strands of her hair.

JoJoJoJoJo...

I shake my head, a single twitch to try and dislodge the thought, and almost slop the wine over the rim of my glass. Leanne shoots me a questioning glance and I smile at her, *All normal here,* just as if I hadn't seen JoJo in my house, hadn't seen Leanne's elder daughter at my work, seen her daughter *screaming.* I think she still knows something is wrong, though, and I push myself to my feet and tell her I'd better shoot.

"Oh, we need to talk about the cake—"

I assure her that it's all in hand, I haven't forgotten. Leanne looks concerned, like the cake shouldn't just be something in my head, not this close to the party, it should pretty much be plated and ready to eat—but of course, it will be. It's on my list, along with writing in her card and picking up the spinning spiral art kit I'm getting for Katie, a gift Leanne picked out for me from the Argos catalogue. I say I'll ring her in the morning, but I've got a couple of things I have to do for work tonight, and I can see she's wondering why I hadn't mentioned them up until now or done them before I came round, but she nods and sees me to the door. I kiss Katie on the head and return her hug and wave goodbye to Chloe, who's still sitting on the sofa, her eyes fixed on me.

The door closes at my back. I walk to Leanne's gate and look up into the sky, but it's too late; the Farleys' spotlight has flicked on, right into my eyes. If there are any stars to be seen, they're lost in the speckles swarming across my vision. For a second, I can't even focus on the latch. I blink and allow my eyesight to adjust, and as I start to open the gate, I see there is someone standing on the other side, a little further down the street.

It's Chloe. She's there, standing between me and my house, and staring at me, just staring, like that; like this morning. As I watch, like a film replaying the same moment, her mouth drops open.

I shake my head. *No.* I just left her behind me. There's no way she can be here, now. Did she run past me while I was dazzled? My hand was on the gate. She'd have to have climbed the fence. She'd have to have *vaulted* it.

Without my noticing? That's impossible.

And this isn't?

I try to tell myself she isn't really here, even while I'm staring at her stricken face, her open mouth. She's wearing her baby pink party top—that's how I'm thinking of it, I realise, her *party top*.

And then I feel angry. This is just another weird hallucination, a product of my mind, that's *all,* and what's it going to do? A vision can't grab hold of me, can't stop me from going home, can't do anything at all. It can't even terrify me unless I let it and I don't know if *this* is the wine now or something else, something inside me, but I'm suddenly determined that it *won't.*

I let the gate slam closed behind me. I walk towards her, my legs moving even as my mind screams at me to *stop,* and then I'm standing right in front of her. I'm the one who could touch her; I could reach out and see if her hair is as real as it looks, and her skin, and those ruffles on her top, but I can't. My resolution is fading away at the sight of the fear in her eyes.

It should help, shouldn't it? It should help, that she's the one who's afraid—but it doesn't.

She's my neighbour's daughter. She's my friend's child and I know I should be asking *What is it Chloe, what's happening Chloe,* but instead I step to the side, towards the parked cars and the road, where I can skirt around her. I glance past her, towards where I want to be—in my home, shut inside—and I see that Shannon is standing a little behind her, further along the pavement.

Shannon stares at me. Just as Chloe is staring at me.

They're playing a trick. The idea is more desperate now than indignant, even though this really would be a mean trick, a cruel trick. It's desperate because I don't know *how*, let alone *why*. And JoJo—how exactly had she played her trick, when she was safely tucked up in bed at home? What had they done, roped her mother into it, too, all of them laughing and laughing?

Shannon has curled her hair. She's wearing too much make-up. She has on white combats and a white crop top, which stand out brightly in the gleam from the Farleys' spotlight. Her mouth is open too, though only a little, not like Chloe's. I don't think she's screaming. I'm not sure how I can tell that because there isn't any sound, it's like I'm in a tunnel and all the air has been squeezed out of it, but Shannon appears to be frozen in shock. If there is a scream, it's silent; it hasn't got past the expression in her eyes.

Then a voice says, "Mrs Thorpe?"

I whirl to see Luke Farley stepping out of his parents' door, past the spotlight, moving from its bright glare into shadow. I wish I could see his features. I want to see if his mouth is hanging open.

"Hi, Mrs Thorpe." He repeats himself, no doubt wondering why I haven't replied. This time the words at least pass through my mind, a kind of reflex: *It's Miss.* I've told him before that I'm a *Miss*, but still he calls me *Mrs* and I know he's trying to be polite, but why should that be the polite thing, anyway? It's as if he thinks *Mrs* is the proper thing to be, the correct thing: marriage, motherhood, all of that, and *Miss* is a demotion, something *less*.

None of that matters, not now. I force myself to say "Hi, Luke," and then neither of us says anything else, and the moment stretches out and the crease that's settled between his eyebrows deepens. It's too old for him, that crease. He's about Chloe's age, though he seems to me the kind of kid who spends most of his time at school in the library, not like her.

He pushes back his fringe, dark and too long, and his gaze flicks towards Chloe's house and returns to me. He looks nervous—he's probably wondering why I'm still standing here, in his way. Because of course, there's nothing to look at. Where Chloe had been, where Shannon had stood, there is nothing but an empty street. He must be wondering why I'm not walking along it and out of his way, so he can go past me to see his friend and they can giggle over what a weirdo Grace Thorpe is, *Miss Thorpe, no wonder she's not married*...

I force myself to walk away. I feel a little unsteady now—*the wine again, that's all it is*—but when I reach my front door, I stop. I think of JoJo. Maybe she'll be inside. I'll walk in and she'll be waiting there in the dark, sitting in that same place on my sofa, staring with those same blank eyes...

I glance over my shoulder and see bright, warm light spilling from Leanne's house. Her door is open and Luke is about to go in. As I watch, he pauses, too. For a moment, he looks over his shoulder, right at me.

Fuck it, I think. I slide my key into the lock, shove the door open, snap out my hand and flick on the light switch. The sofa is empty. So is the room. Of course it is. My whole fucking house is empty. My *life* is empty.

I close the door behind me and wonder what Luke is saying right now, to Chloe, to Leanne, to my best friends in the world. I comfort myself with the thought that Chloe, beautiful, bright Chloe, is about a thousand miles out of Luke Farley's league. Perhaps I'm beginning to understand her *Oh-em-gees* and *As ifs* and *No ways*. Does he really imagine, for one second, that he could be her boyfriend? Well, bless him.

I know I'm the one being mean now, and I don't care. It's not like there's any need for tricks. It's not like Luke Farley ever stood a chance.

CHAPTER FOUR
Two Days to the Party

It's Thursday. I'm supposed to be working from home, reviewing budgets for a big project, but instead I'm here, in a moderately-sized Sainsbury's. I've already been and picked up Katie's present; now I have a basket over my arm and in it, a caterpillar cake and some striped birthday candles. I was expecting the caterpillar to be called Colin or something like that, but apparently here it's called Giggles and it's very suitably pink. I'm picturing it cut into slices. Trying to recount the names of everyone who will be at the party. Katie, of course. Daisy and Ruby and Isla, I remember them. Chloe and Shannon—will they want cake? And me, though I needn't have any. And JoJoJoJoJo...

Chloe and Shannon and JoJo, all in one place together. The three of them.

I shake my head, pushing away the images that rise, returning to the present, to reality. Will it be enough? Perhaps I ought to get *two* caterpillar cakes. Would that look odd? Dad would have just shoved them together on a plate, and it's not like I'd have minded. I could get clever, put something green beneath them to look like grass. Icing—would I have to make the icing, or can I buy that, too? Maybe broken biscuits, to look like soil.

I'm reaching for a packet of Digestives when my mobile rings. I've left the volume turned up in case anyone calls from work, but it's Leanne's name that appears on the screen. I swipe to answer, almost elbowing some guy who's half-blocking the aisle, and put it to my ear, remembering as I do so that I'd said I'd call her.

"Hey!" I manage to speak first. "You had a houseful last night! I saw Luke on my way back. He took me by surprise. And what with the girls, Shannon, me... sorry I had to dash." I'm rattling on, hoping my words explain away any oddness Luke might have mentioned; standing there, staring into space, seeing things. *Took me by surprise.* Is that enough?

"Shannon?" Leanne sounds surprised. "She wasn't here. Yeah, Luke was a bit unexpected! But I was calling about—"

Shit. I talk over her, trying to cover my mistake, something else to smooth over. "Ah sorry, of course. Don't mind me, I was thinking of the *other* night. So busy just now, the days are blurring into one!"

"Speaking of which—"

"Don't worry, Lee, I'm on the case. Does Katie like caterpillars? I'm picking one up right now. A cake, I mean."

A puzzled silence reaches from her end of the line to mine. "Oh—weren't you making one? I thought you'd said you were." A pause. "It's fine, of course, anything—it's good of you, Grace. You really don't have to buy one, though. I might have said to Katie—"

Her voice tails away.

"Trust me, this one will be much better than anything I'd make." I laugh.

"It's just, she was so looking forward. I mean, she'll eat any cake, obviously! Only when you said—*I* said—I told her you were making it especially, because you're her special aunt, and because you—"

Because you love her. That's what she was about to say; she doesn't need to finish. And I hear the words: *And because she loves you too.*

I can see the expression Leanne must have on her face right at this moment. It's the same one I saw her wear once before. What was it she'd said that time? *Grace, where is she? You haven't* left *her—*

Suddenly I'm angry. Here I am again, failing again, at being a *mum*, when I'm not a fucking mum, I never even *had* a mum, I don't even know how that goes actually, *Leanne*, and I'm shocked at the way the words rush in and circle my brain, so much sharper and more raw than I'd known they could be, a flock of crows ready to jab and rend.

For a moment, I don't say anything. I take a deep breath, then another. I adopt a bright tone and say, "Of course I will. I'll bake one. How hard can it be?"

Leanne dissolves into exclamations and enthusiasm. She's all *Can you really?* And *That will be perfect, thanks so much Grace, you're such a star, Grace*, and before it's time to ring off, it's enough to make me smile. I shove the cake back onto the shelf—*Sorry, Giggles*—and whirl around to head for the baking section, almost bashing into the same man, still standing in the aisle. He probably doesn't know what he wants, he's as clueless as I am, poor sod, and I see that he's not even facing the produce. He's got his back to all the tins and packets, as if he's ground to a halt, probably waiting for his wife to join him and give him a nudge and set him moving again. I mutter an apology, though I'm already googling ingredients for Victoria sponge. Will Katie like Victoria sponge? Will Ruby and Daisy and JoJo? I have no idea. Don't kids like every kind of cake?

I think of Giggles. Chocolate! Everyone loves chocolate, don't they? I search for that instead and add cocoa powder to my mental list. Eggs, flour, sugar, baking powder, and milk—I've got some of that, but better buy extra. All I have in my basket now is that little box of candles. I have no idea where half this stuff is. I raise my head to give the lost man a look of shared sympathy, and I see the way he's glaring at me, and everything stops.

"Uh—h—" *Hello, that's the word you're looking for*, I tell my brain, but it doesn't help. Those eyes won't let me say it or even think it. This man is not especially tall but he's stocky, and broad with it; beer gut, muscular shoulders, hunched posture, hardly any neck. There's a hardness in his eyes, like he's had things rough and still carries them somewhere close to the surface. There's a whiff of neglect about him, of not caring, like he'd started shopping and then just couldn't be bothered to carry on. Or maybe it's because he saw me, and something about the sight made him angry—

—*so* angry. He goes on glaring at me. Glaring and glaring.

I cast my mind back. I'd almost jostled him, but I hadn't made contact, had I? I'm pretty sure I didn't. My phone had rung and distracted me. Is that what he's taken exception to—the volume of my ring tone, my conversation? He doesn't look like the type to bother about that and it's not as if I'd talked for long. Hell, it's not as if we're in the sodding cinema.

I'd apologised before; I'm not doing so again. I grab a little carton of baking powder and shove it into my basket and stride onwards before realising I've forgotten the bloody cocoa. I turn back, raising my gaze just enough to see that he hasn't moved, not one inch. I can still feel his eyes on me and when I've got the cocoa I decide I'm not avoiding him, I'm not scared, why should I be? I decide to meet his look, but when I turn again—

He's gone.

I stare along the aisle, judging how long it would take for someone to get to the end and pass out of sight. I start along it myself. I peer down the next aisle, and the one on the other side. He isn't in either of them.

I hurry right to the end of the shop and scan the self-service tills on one side and the staffed counter on the other. I peer out through the glass windows, trying to spot him walking away. *Not there, not there, not there.*

I try to tell myself he's found his wife, that he's simply been prodded into action, but I can't persuade myself that's true. If he'd walked away, I'd have heard his steps on the hard floor. I'd have sensed his movement. He isn't here because he never was here, and that's the truth of it. I rub my eyes, as if that will fix anything, and I focus on the young woman standing behind the checkout. She's running the end of her ginger plait through her fingers and watching me.

I don't care for the look she gives me any more than I had the stranger's, but at least I can understand it. There's something a little like amusement in her eyes, and I know what she's thinking; I can practically see the thought in her head.

Visions of Grace

Mad bitch.

She doesn't even know why I'm looking around this way. If she knew what I thought I'd just seen, what I've *been* seeing—what then?

JoJo, I think. *And Chloe and Shannon.* Somehow the voice in my head is Katie's, reciting the names. Now there's this man. Not someone who was in my head, in my thoughts, but a complete stranger.

Why would I see a complete stranger?

A balloon, floating up into the sky.

A birthday party in less than a week.

My phone goes off, making me jump. It's a weird thing, but it's only in that moment that my heartbeat fires up, like a car going from nought to sixty in too little time. I raise it in front of me and see that work is calling. They probably want to know why the hell I haven't signed off the figures yet for their oh-so important pitch. I swipe to send the call to voicemail. I still have to buy half the things on my list. Sugar, eggs, flour, such very ordinary, everyday things. *Mum* things. But first I stand there, allowing my heart rate to subside, trying so very hard to turn myself back into something ordinary, too.

Once I'm home again, I dump the shopping bags on the worktop in the kitchen and leave them where they are. I go into the lounge, fire up my laptop and call up the spreadsheet I should have been looking at. I run my eyes over the figures—they look right, but they won't seem to stay in one place, in their tidy little columns and rows. What do they even matter?

My mind returns to the things I've seen. *JoJo and Chloe and Shannon. JoJo and Chloe and Shannon.* I'm still hearing their names in Katie's voice. It's not her full invitation list, of course not, but it still seems connected to the party, somehow. A pink balloon; a pink ruffled top; a little girl's party dress. I try to think of the other names: Daisy and Ruby come to mind. Isla, too. And Em, that was it. An Emma or an Emily, maybe an Emmeline or something else like that. Not so many. Some mums have whole classes attend their kids' birthdays, don't they? But there are enough, just right for Leanne's house, the same shape and size and layout as mine.

I picture a bunch of little girls, wearing their very best party dresses and their very best smiles, all in some variation of pink, and Chloe and Shannon and Leanne, and between them, hovering at their shoulders, appearing in the spaces between the names that Katie goes on and on chanting in my mind, *him*: a dark shadow with a hunched form and a hard expression. A matching coldness in his eyes; a *dead* expression. The only one whose name I don't know.

Who are you? I think. *Who?*

No answer comes. No memory rises to match his form, his features, his expression. There is not even the most distant chiming of a bell.

I have never seen him before.

A stranger, then. *Stranger danger.*

A balloon, floating into the air.

Happy Birthday!

It all seems to come back to that. JoJo and Shannon and Chloe—Chloe who was *screaming*, don't forget, *screaming*—will all be at that party. Yes, there'll be a bunch of other little girls, ones I don't know—but will there also be someone else? Someone who shouldn't be there, who wasn't invited, isn't welcome?

Or perhaps he *is* invited, and I just don't know it yet. It's not like I can demand to vet Leanne's invitation list. Maybe she's invited Ruby's father, or Em's. Or she's stuck to the mums, only one of them will bring some uncle along, *Oh, look who happened to call in.* Or he'll be some other friend.

Katie's dad isn't in our lives any more.

The memory lands in my brain, whole and complete. The way Leanne had shrugged off all thought of him, as if he was some mistake she'd once made and nothing more.

I think of the man I'd seen in Sainsbury's, dark and broad and frowning. I try to imagine him as anyone's dad. I try to picture him with Leanne. It's hard to do, but perhaps that's why she'd felt the whole thing was a mistake. I try to envision him with Katie, her in a clean pink dress, sitting in his lap, and I shudder.

But it wasn't Katie I saw. It was JoJo...

My thoughts circle back. Could JoJo and her family know the man? Maybe he doesn't always look that way. Maybe, with a shave and a change of clothes, even a smile, he might appear altogether different.

I still can't see it. I can't imagine that's true. I can't believe he was ever with Leanne or any of her friends.

I think he's as much a stranger to Leanne, to Katie, to JoJo and Chloe and Shannon, as he is to me.

Kids know all about *stranger danger* these days, don't they? My dad used to let me play out until dark when I was little, me and my mates running or cycling around pretty much wherever we wanted, but it isn't like that now. Mums keep a closer watch. There are too many stories in the news. Children snatched from gardens, from back yards. What do they teach them to do or say now—to run away? To point at the stranger and scream? I don't know, I'm not a mum, but they must have some kind of plan.

And I have no idea what to do. All I have is *me*, seeing things, things that patently aren't there, that are impossible. Still, it feels as if they are coalescing somehow, taking on a new and ugly shape, one I don't want to look at. As if I'm being haunted by something that hasn't happened yet, seeing ghosts of people who aren't—

They're not dead.

I feel sick. Those things that happen on television or in the papers, to other people's kids, they're not going to happen to my friends, or their friends...

They're not ghosts. JoJo and Chloe and Shannon aren't ghosts, they'll never be ghosts, because they're fine.

Yet I must be seeing these things for a reason. I have to be.

Suddenly, the time in front of me seems very short. Soon, Katie will be leaping out of bed, *all excited like she thinks it's her birthday already*, except this time it will be, it's here, and she'll get up at dawn and rip open her big pile of presents and have ice cream for breakfast if she wants to, and soon, soon, she will see her friends...

My friends, too. People I *love*.

I feel something else, then. Something like determination deep inside me, like storm-clouds gathering in the sky. Something strong and implacable and fiercely protective.

Is this what a mother feels like?

I sit here on my sofa, right in the place where JoJo had been, and I close my eyes. When I open them, the screen of my laptop swims in and out of focus. I pull it towards me and, with a couple of swipes, I sign off on the figures. *Done.* Of course they'll be okay. Our project managers know what they're doing. When are they ever *not* okay?

I will be ready. I'm going to be at that party. And everything will be okay there, too. I'll just have to see that it is. I don't know how I'm going to do that—I can't see that far, not yet—but for now, I will do this.

I'm going to bake a sodding cake.

A few hours later, it's ready, filling my kitchen with warming, chocolatey smells. It wasn't that difficult, when it came down to it. Just a matter of taking one step after another until it was finished: perfect, round, nicely risen.

Yet I'd so nearly messed it up. Even with all my googling and preparation it almost went horribly wrong, but still, I took action and I fixed it. The thing I hadn't bloody thought of, not once, is that I don't possess any cake tins. It was a crucial piece I'd been missing, but I found a way around it. I couldn't admit my omission to Leanne, didn't want to give her anything to worry about just now except Katie, so I nipped over the road to the Farleys' and asked if I could borrow some. Gemma Farley is one of those mums who's all sleek ponytail and yoga tops, the kind whose lid always fits neatly on her glass box on recycling day. Sure enough, she had about a dozen baking tins, all in different sizes. Even Luke, hovering in a corner, rolled his eyes at the sight of them while she helped me pick out a couple and extricated them from the rest.

Now Katie has her cake. My reason to be at the party is all set. Soon, when it's cooled, I will add buttercream and pour melted chocolate on top. It'll look a little bit messy, but why the hell not? Katie will be able to tell I've made it with my own hands, made it with love, her special aunt, and I'll have the candles ready to press into it and my voice primed to sing *Happy birthday*. Then, those things taken care of, I will do the next thing, and the next, to make sure that whatever happens, whatever it is I'm *seeing*, doesn't happen at all.

As for that man, that stranger—he'd just better stay the hell away from us.

Oddly, as if from nowhere—or perhaps like another message, reaching me from the universe perhaps, or karma, or fate, or wherever such things come from—a memory rises, and my father's voice floats into my mind.

We always knew you were special, Grace. Just as soon as we saw you.

My mother had been long gone by then. I was in my teens, and I'd had a difficult day at school. I was crying, I remember that. I'd been picked last for a team at netball, then, as if to prove my classmates right, I'd been so clumsy: dropping the ball, missing easy passes, tripping over my own feet. They had laughed at me. *Not so graceful, are you?* And so I'd gone home and asked my dad why they'd called me Grace.

You were like—a gift. A little Angel. Like you'd been—bestowed on us.

Dad didn't speak that way, not ever. We only ever talked about what time he'd pick me up or what was for tea or what we'd watch on telly, not things that mattered, not then. I remember the way he'd hesitated over the word *bestowed*, like he was embarrassed to use it, but he'd said it anyway, and I'd been so glad.

I realised then that Dad had never meant *Grace* as in physical movement. He—and my mum—had meant something else when they named me. A line I'd read somewhere came to me then: *Angels and ministers of grace defend us...* I'd thought it was from Shakespeare, though in that moment it had felt almost biblical.

Grace. You mean like in church? I had asked.

Well, I don't rightly know, love. We never really went to church, did we? Dad had chuckled then, and the moment was gone, but it had been there: *bestowed.* And it's here in front of me now. It's here for a reason.

Angels and ministers of grace defend us.

And I will. If there was ever anything special in me, one shred of Grace in my body, I will be special for Katie. And Chloe. And Shannon. And for JoJo.

Chapter Five
One Day to the Party

The trouble starts mid-morning.

I'm at work, in the office this time and at my desk, and Sue is making the coffees. Neil sits back with his hands tucked behind his head, the sprung back of his seat rocking slightly with his movement. The phone shrills into life on my desk, and I pick it up and the managing director's voice says, "Grace. Could I have a minute?"

That doesn't sound good, even before he rings off without another word. Carlisle is a hands-off kind of M.D., and if he wants something from my department he usually goes through Neil. I'm oddly calm as I replace the handset—too calm. I stand and walk up the aisle towards the office in the corner, the only one with actual walls around it. I knock, hear a single terse syllable—*Come*—and go in. Harry, one of the project managers, is already seated in front of Carlisle's broad desk, and I know at once what this is about.

I see again the way I'd signed off those figures. *When are they ever* not *okay?*

It seems that now is the time.

Carlisle doesn't tell me to take a seat. He launches right into it. How Harry had forgotten to copy the material costs for the secondary construction into the file and *How the hell had I missed that?* Harry works his jaw and stares down at the grey carpet tiles, not meeting my eye, because it's Harry who's messed up but at least he's spotted his own mistake. I hadn't, and now the pitch has been sent, and there's no way we can honour the quote. We'd lose a fortune. All we can do is hike it and lose face or withdraw and lose face, and don't I realise this is my *job*?

I agree that it is, and apologise in the right places, and feel like I'm shrinking into the floor while Harry goes on and on not looking at me. I keep waiting for the words, *You're fired*, but they don't come, and somehow I realise that's all this is: a ticking off, a warning shot, and I also know it doesn't matter. Quotes and projects and numbers and work—none of that matters.

A little girl with dark brown hair and a smile that matches her very best friend's. Two young women just finding their way in the world, in possession of all the beauty of youth and with all the confidence and happiness that comes from that. They are what matters.

I make it out of Carlisle's office, assuring him I'll do better, and knowing that I will, after all of this is over, and I hardly look where I'm going. I only come to a halt when I almost walk into someone.

A man's chest is right in front of me. The shirt is off-white, like it's been worn for a couple of days, and I can see the outline of a vest underneath it. There's no tie, only a couple of inches of wiry hair where the top button's been left open and somehow I *know*, even as I raise my head. My knees are going, I feel them turning to something loose and unstable and it's him, it's him, it's *him*.

I'm so sure he'll be there that I can already see him looking back at me. Hatred in his eyes. I feel I could reach out and touch him. My fingers twitch with the foreknowledge of grimy cotton and unwashed skin and coarse dark hair. He's as real as I am, as real as Carlisle or Harry or Neil. I feel like I can't breathe but I hear the air going in and out of me, shallow and fast. I try to summon that sense of determination, of fearlessness, but inside, I'm the one who's screaming.

I blink and look up again and he isn't there—but still, he *is*.

Visions of Grace

I tell myself I'm not afraid of him—but I *am*.

My eyes are staring. I can't see his face, and yet I do, every moment. The potential of him. The knowledge that he could appear now, or now, or *now*.

I feel a hand on my arm and whirl to see Sue, and realise, to my horror, that I'm saying the words out loud. "You're there. I know you're there. I *know*…"

Sue's lips are moving too, but there seems to be a delay before her words reach me, as if we're on some long-distance phone call. I recognise their shape, though, and I know that she's saying my name, over and over. *Grace… Grace… Grace*. It's like before, the word hardly seems like *me* any longer, it's more like a *thing* she's talking about, or maybe a plea…

"Sit down, love," she says then. I'm not at my desk, but she turfs the nearest staff member—Alex—out of his chair and spins it towards me. "Are you all right? You had me worried there for a minute. You looked like you'd seen a ghost."

A ghost. That makes me want to laugh. *That's not what he is*, I want to say, *Not what any of them are*, but I bite back the words. She wouldn't understand. How could she?

Sue calls out for Neil. He's our boss, but she's telling him to bring me tea, to put plenty of sugar in it. "You can drink it in a minute, love. Then I think you should go home, don't you? When you feel a bit better."

Before Neil vanishes, he nods. *Yes, you should*. They've already decided without me. And that suits me just fine.

Inside half an hour, I'm driving away. Now that it's over, my cheeks are burning. My hands shake on the steering wheel. I glance up into the sky as I pull out of the car park, looking for a pink balloon: *Happy Birthday!* I don't see one. The sky is starting to spit with rain. There's only grey reality, closing in like a coffin lid.

At least my heartbeat feels somewhere near normal again. Everything around me is normal too, people walking down the street, hunched under umbrellas or into their macs. A bus disgorges its passengers—I find myself looking for *him* among them, but I don't see him anywhere. Then I realise I'm about to pass the little Sainsbury's with its cheery orange sign.

Before I can think about it, I've yanked the car towards the turning and into the car park and come to a stop. I'm glad no one's about to look at me as I sit there gathering myself, simply breathing. Still, I can't put him out of my mind. That grimy, once-white shirt, that wiry hair. The bulk of him, the physicality. And that sense of anger, the neglect leaching from him, like he's lived his whole life outside the bounds of whatever normality is.

The cold, hard light in his eyes. The darkness, under the surface of him.

I wonder if he's in the shop again, back where I first saw him. Just standing there.

I step out of the car, glance around and walk to the entrance. Grabbing a basket, I scan what I can see of the aisles then walk towards the baking shelf, just as if I've been picking it clean all my life. I throw my head back as I turn the corner and see right down the aisle and it is blessedly empty, and it feels a little bit like grace, like something *bestowed*. I don't need anything, not now—my cake is ready—but I pick up some silver balls to put on top. I'm not sure they go with chocolate, but I don't care.

Feeling as if I'm challenging him, I go to the party section at the end of the aisle. There's a packet of balloons; not metallic, not pink, but red and yellow and blue. I add those to my basket. Then streamers, extra wrapping paper, picnic plates with teddy bears on them, plastic knives and forks, everything. I practically empty the shelf. Leanne will have all this already, but that doesn't matter either. It will show how much I care. How prepared I am, how like a mum.

When I'm finished, I turn my back on the produce and stop dead in the middle of the aisle. It takes me a moment to raise my head. I tell myself

I'm ready. That it's a good thing, if I do see him. I can *use* it. I'll use it to fix his features ever more firmly in my mind, so that I'll know him when I see him again, when I see him for *real*...

The man isn't there. Not in the corner, not at my elbow, not standing behind me.

I go over to a stand of greetings cards. There's one with a pink number 6 on it. I've already bought one but it doesn't have Katie's age on it, so I'll get this instead. I can give her the other next year. Or maybe JoJo, when it's her turn.

He still hasn't appeared. I glance around, then behind me once more. *Not there, not there, not there.*

He isn't anywhere.

But if he can see me, he'll know I'm not about to slink off like a frightened rabbit. Never again. I can't let him think that. He has to know that he should be the one to turn around, to run away, to never come back.

I grab a pack of fun-size Mars Bars. A box of lemon slices. Another of chocolate fingers. I throw in giant bags of Monster Munch and Wotsits. My breath is shallow. My hands are still shaking. I glance around me, behind me, expecting him to appear at my shoulder, at my back, over in the corner, louring, brooding, *threatening*. But he doesn't. Perhaps he can sense my mood. Perhaps I've scared him off.

"Aw," says the lady behind the till as she empties my basket, passing item after item through the barcode reader. She has grey hair and glasses secured on a chain around her neck. The girl with the ginger plait and the stare is nowhere to be seen, and I feel my shoulders start to relax. "Six!" she says, seeing the card. "Lovely age. My granddaughter's eleven now. Flies by, doesn't it?"

I glance down at the items, at all the pink and the sugar and the happiness, and I open my mouth to tell her *She's not mine*, but what would be the point? I smile and agree that it does. "She's so excited," I find myself saying. "Keeps getting up at dawn!"

"I'll bet." She indicates the card reader and waits for me to swipe. "Thank you. And many happy returns to—"

"Katie," I smile back, taking hold of my bags. "Her name is Katie. She can't wait for her birthday."

Chapter Six
The Day of the Party

I wake up and the image of Katie leaping out of bed is so vivid, I hear her voice as if it's in the next room. "It's today!" she shouts, so excited, diving into a pile of pink-wrapped presents, all the things she could ever want. I remind myself that will already have happened. She'll have been up for hours, will have dragged Leanne out of bed and ripped them all open by now. Maybe she's insisted on wearing her party dress, far too early, but so what? It's her birthday.

Soon she'll open the door and find all her friends waiting there: Ruby and Isla, Em and Daisy, and JoJo, of course, her very best friend. Chloe and Shannon will be there too, all wearing the same wide, brilliant smiles. And between them—will there be a taller, darker shape that shouldn't be there—a shadow?

I shake my head, trying to fight back the headache already gathering behind my eyes. I close them and see a birthday cake, not perfect or even especially neat, but made with love, candles pressed into it, cracking the thick chocolate spread over the top, silver balls rolling off and bouncing from the plate. It's my mother's china, with little blue flowers around the rim, though it's my hands I see holding it. The candles are lit, and I hear the drift of voices; everyone singing for Katie, who is waiting in the middle of them, all wearing those smiles, wide and red.

Suddenly, they're gone. I see a buffet table picked bare, shreds of wrapping paper and discarded party hats, chairs abandoned, overturned; and my cake, that took so much effort, the work of my hands, is on the floor. The sponge is in pieces, crumbs everywhere, along with smashed crockery and scattered candles. One of those candles is still lit. It smoulders, an angry flickering, as if it is only now beginning to burn.

I press my hands to my eyes and lights flicker behind the lids, darting this way and that as I rub them; small, cold flames only I can put out.

It's today! I think. I force myself to step out of bed and get into the shower. When I'm done, I wipe a smeary line of condensation from the mirror and stare into it. My reflection is blurry around the edges but I can still make out my pasty skin, pouchy eyes, limp hair. Everything about me looks tired, although if anything, my eyes are a little too bright. I lean closer, peer into them. They have nothing to show me I haven't already seen, and I tell myself I'm ready.

Like Katie as I've pictured her, I'm in my party clothes way too early, like an overgrown, over-excited birthday girl. No pink frock for me; I'd planned to wear a cerise wrap dress, but I might need to move quickly, even to run. Who knows? If I do, I'll be ready, in my jeans and a lacy blouse.

I sit on the sofa and nurse a cup of tea, unable to stomach the idea of breakfast. I try to think of what food I could manage and all that springs to mind is a slice of chocolate cake: gooey, rich, a thick crust of melted Cadbury's across the top. Well, that's not happening. I realise I'm sitting right where JoJo had. The thought of seeing her again today, seeing her for real, makes me queasy. Chloe, too, of course, and Shannon.

It's only then that I think: *Why haven't I done something about Chloe and Shannon?*

It's not like they're six years old. It's not as if they'd really want to be at a little girl's party. Couldn't I have tried to stop them from going? Now they'll be thrown together with JoJo, probably with a pink metallic birthday balloon hovering over their heads, and something will happen. I know that. I've known it for days. Why didn't I speak to Leanne? I could have told her not to invite JoJo. I could have treated Chloe and Shannon to a day out, bought them tickets for something else, something they couldn't resist.

But Leanne would never have excluded Katie's very best friend. And Chloe loves her sister; of course she'll want to be at her party. If I'd tried to interfere, they would have looked at me like I was mad. Possibly *I'd* have been the one to find myself uninvited.

And I'm the one who most needs to be there. Today, I'm the very best friend any of them could ever have.

I push myself up, go into the kitchen and pour granola into a bowl. I have to eat. I can't be feeling faint later, might be grateful for the strength. As I eat, bowl in hand, I wander to the front window. I peer along the street, where all I see is the neighbours' houses, neighbours' cars. A cat that's been exploring the Farleys' yard leaps the wall, trots across the road, slips behind a van and out of sight. There's no other movement, no one standing around, no one who shouldn't be there. No *shadow*.

Ten minutes later, I check again. Then I give up all pretence that I'm not watching for someone. I fetch a stool from the kitchen, place it close to the window and sit right next to the glass. Now I can see anyone who walks by or drives up the road. I don't move until lunchtime, when I make a sandwich, forcing myself to swallow the bread, which seems so dry it makes my throat sore. I gulp down water, telling myself I don't feel sick.

Eventually, a car makes its way slowly up the street. It stops by the kerb outside Leanne's house. A woman is driving and a little girl sits behind her. Not JoJo; this child has fair hair, though I can't properly make her out. Only that she's wearing a voluminous, shiny top.

No: not a top. It's a balloon. She's clutching it in front of her: a pink balloon. It's in the shape of a heart.

There, I think. *There you are.*

I realise I've got to my feet, without consciously knowing I was going to move. I'm not even sure if I muttered the words out loud. I don't have to look at my watch; it's half an hour before the party's supposed to start, but that doesn't matter. I should have got there first. Leanne isn't expecting me yet, but so what? She'll be glad to see me, glad of the extra help. I could have been keeping an eye on the road from her house as well as from mine.

I grab the things I need and practically run out of the house. The little girl and her mum are nowhere to be seen, must have already gone inside.

They've left their balloon attached to Leanne's front door.

I find I can hardly breathe at the sight of it. I stare, as if it's some nemesis I've found waiting for me and not a child's cheerful party balloon. Here it is, pulling and bobbing on its string, as if it already wants to fly. *Happy Birthday!* it says. And there, beneath, that big number *6*.

Right here, a vision made real. Here, where anyone can see. Telling anyone, everyone, that the birthday girl is inside: a little innocent six-year-old and her friends, having a party. I balance the things I'm holding in my arms. In one hand: the cake, covered in cling-film. Katie's gift-wrapped art set is tucked under my arm, and two carrier bags of paper plates and biscuits and sweets and crisps are cutting into my elbow. Visions of smashed china or not, I have placed the cake on one of my mother's old plates. It's precious to me, yes—but it feels like kind of a spell, or perhaps a wish: *Be here for me.* If ever a mother's love was needed, that simple, everyday magic, it is now.

With my free hand, I take hold of the balloon's string. It looks as if they've just wound it around the door handle...

The door opens. The string tugs from my fingers. Leanne stands in the gap, already looking harassed. She appears puzzled for a second to see me here so early, then she smiles. She opens her mouth to greet me, but the words "Aaaaaauntie Graaaace!" replace her own and Katie is there, bobbing up and down, like—*like a balloon,* unable to stand still.

"I got roller skates Auntie Grace and nail stickers and friendship bracelets and a unicorn and a princess dress!" she shouts, without pausing between words.

I stare at the metallic heart shape still jiggling from the door handle—

Visions of Grace

but what can I do? Pop it? Snatch it away? They'll think I'm mad. I can't have that, I need to help them. I need to be *one* of them—

So I laugh and indicate the present under my arm. "You'd better open this, too!"

Katie whoops, relieves me of the gift and runs off, floomping down on the sofa. There's another little girl already sitting there, and a woman I don't know. She tells me she's Jess, Isla's mum, but she's just going. I say goodbye to her and hello to Isla and there's another knock at the door. I use that as an excuse to peek out of the window, but all I see is a bunch of little girls crowded into the yard. Then Ruby and Daisy are here, and Em, who tells me her name is Emma, and Katie has more gifts and everyone's saying hello and mums who aren't staying are saying *See you later* and Katie is shrieking, and I blink against the sound. I'm trying to breathe steadily, but my heart is beating hard in my chest, letting me know it's there, telling me *it's time*.

I touch Leanne lightly on the shoulder and tell her not to mind me, I'm going to make myself useful. I go into the kitchen where the worktops are covered with plates of sandwiches and sausage rolls and pieces of quiche and slices of pizza, all covered with cling film. I set down the cake and start unpacking crisps and sweets, though there's hardly room for it all. Leanne comes in halfway through to pour lemonade into paper cups.

"Oh Grace, that's kind. You really shouldn't have." She gives me a smile, a real one this time. "Sorry, I'll maybe get us something stronger later."

"There's no need." I can't be drinking, I need to stay sharp. "Have you had a good morning?"

"Exhausting already! I mean, Katie's loving it. That's the main thing." For a moment she looks unhappy, like there's something she wants to tell me, or perhaps doesn't, then she says, "We got a card from Katie's dad."

Everything in me goes quiet. "Oh?"

The bottle of lemonade thuds to the counter; she seems to have forgotten it. "Of all the things," she says. "He's never bothered—I mean, he's never been with us—and then, *boom*. Just like that."

I speak carefully. "That must have been confusing for Katie."

"Ah. Well, it would have been. I haven't showed her. I mean, I suppose I will. I'll have to, won't I. Will I?" She shakes her head. "I can't even think about it now."

"No, of course." I murmur the words, but even while she's telling me thank you, that I'm a good friend, maybe we can talk it over with a proper drink some time, and I'm nodding, I'm picturing a man: broad, unkempt, glaring. Someone I had tried to imagine with a little girl in his lap and couldn't. I look at Leanne's hair, freshly cut; at her neat, pale pink shift dress. I still can't picture them together, but then, she'd told me he was never really in their lives. Perhaps that's why; because he was never really suitable, didn't fit in. Or maybe he'd only become that way afterwards, when he'd felt the loss of them...

I can't rule anything out, not now. Stranger things happen. Look at me and Connor; we were together for years. I never could imagine us being apart, but that happened too, didn't it? The last thing I'd heard, he's with someone else. Married. Last thing I'd heard, they've had a baby together.

Leanne finishes pouring the drinks. She grasps three paper cups by their rims, well-practised, three more in the other hand, and carries them off. *Six.* One too many, so far, anyway, but never mind.

I wander over to her kitchen shelves, where framed photographs sit alongside jars and mugs and rows of glass tumblers. I look over each one. Could he have been here in front of me, all the time? But of course he isn't. It won't be that easy. The pictures show the three of them, over and over: at a theme park, posing in front of the London Eye, sitting on a beach. There's no man in any of them.

Some of Katie's drawings are stuck to the fridge with magnets and I check those, too, already knowing it's hopeless. She doesn't know her dad, and it's not like she can capture a likeness, not at her age. Still, I don't think there's a man in any of those, either. It's like before; only girls, some taller, some shorter, scribbled hair, triangles for skirts, all with those same red grins.

Visions of Grace

I need to check outside again. The pavements, the road. See who might be coming.

Back in the lounge, the girls are sitting in a circle on the floor. Leanne's put on some music, jaunty and happy, *Saturday Night*, but the chatter is louder still. I wish they weren't so loud. My headache intensifies even as the thought floats through my mind.

Katie looks up and I blink.

She doesn't look like Katie any longer. It's like she's turned into one of her drawings. *Red grin, red grin, red grin.*

But Katie is smiling, she isn't hurt, and I realise that the girls are painting their faces. Or rather, they're putting on make-up, kids' make-up. There's a pile of glitter eye shadows in the middle of the circle, along with pastel-coloured palettes and little sponge applicators. The girls' eyes are streaked blue or green or both and pink spots adorn their cheeks, and all of their lips are red, red, red. Those mouths stretch and grin and leer at me. I force myself to smile, to act like nothing is wrong, trying to quell my unease at the sight. Then I think: *Aren't there too many?*

I focus on a figure I recognise. Pink flared dress, white patterned tights. Grinning up at me, red, red smeared all over her lips. It's JoJo. She's appeared just like that, like an apparition, like a *ghost*. She's grinning and grinning. Katie nudges her in the ribs and they put their heads together and giggle. Thick as thieves. Co-conspirators.

I shake my head. I've been watching, yet I'd never seen her arrive. Never heard the door open while I lingered in the kitchen. But Leanne poured six cups of lemonade. Just the right number, being efficient, just as if JoJo was always here, has always been here...

I squeeze my eyes closed for a moment. JoJo must have stayed the night with her friend, that's all. A special treat for the birthday girl and her very best friend. She *was* already here. There's nothing strange about it, unless it's in the way I'm standing here, staring at them.

It's a relief to turn my back and draw the curtain aside. I check the path outside, the garden, the drive, the road.

"We're all here." Leanne's voice, just behind me, makes me jump. "Chloe and Shannon are upstairs."

I open my mouth to reply with something noncommittal—*Ah, okay, fine*—when there comes a knock at the door.

Leanne looks at me, puzzled, as if I have the answer, but I don't. Whoever it is must have been standing right behind the door. I hadn't seen a sign of them.

Leanne goes to answer. Katie stares up at me with her bloody-looking lips. All the girls do, and Chloe and Shannon come bounding down the stairs, wearing exactly what I knew they'd be wearing, and I also know before it happens that everything is about to go wrong. I wait for that man to appear, to push his way inside—but Leanne is smiling, she's letting him in, and it isn't the stranger at all but Luke, holding out a card and a packet of party rings.

Chloe's voice cuts through the air. "What are you doing here?" I notice her shaking Shannon off; her friend is clinging to her arm, snorting with laughter.

"Chloe, don't be rude." Leanne reaches out and takes the card. "That's very thoughtful of you, love."

Luke hardly seems to have heard Leanne, or he's ignoring her. It's like Chloe is all he can see. He tries to speak airily but doesn't quite manage it. "Oh, I'm just dropping a card in for the birthday girl."

Chloe isn't impressed; her gaze doesn't soften. She draws herself tall, taller than he is. She's wearing that pink ruffled top and some white jeans that look painted on. She's as leggy as a gazelle. As haughty as she is beautiful.

Luke, as if desperate to explain his presence, glances around and settles on me. "We helped make Katie's cake," he says. "So I had to wish her happy birthday, didn't I?"

I stare. They didn't help, not really, they only lent me a couple of cake tins, but when I feel everyone turning towards me I force a tight-lipped smile. Luke shouldn't be here. He's only going to get in the way, someone else I'll have to think about. Yet he wouldn't even know about this party if it wasn't for me, would he? I'm changing things already. Maybe that's a good thing. Maybe I've changed them enough that today will be just what it's supposed to be, a simple, fun, child's party, and Katie will fall into bed at the end of it and Leanne will tuck her in, and everything will be fine.

Leanne thanks him again, exclaiming over Luke doing all that. She steps back and draws him into the room, asks if he wants a drink. She suggests he might not want to stay, kids' birthday parties being what they are, but it seems that Luke does. Maybe he's hoping for the expression in Chloe's eyes to soften, or for her to at least look at him. His gaze keeps going to her and sliding away.

The door closes behind him. He congratulates Katie on being six years old.

It isn't like I'd thought, having a kids' party. It isn't how I'd imagined. Or rather, it's *more*. I knew there'd be noise, but still: there's so *much*. It's all yelling and shrieking and shouts. It's jangly kids' music that won't let up. It's a headache lit in disco lights, throbbing behind my eyes. My attention skips from one thing to another, *this* and *this* and then *this*. There's only a handful of kids here, and I can't imagine what it'd be like if there were more of them. If they'd had the whole class along, classes and clowns and God knows what else. I don't really know.

I keep checking the window. Outside, nothing seems to change. The day is quiet and grey. I watch for figures hiding behind cars or standing very still in the shadows.

Could it be that someone is there, but they've seen me first, seen me watching and are avoiding my gaze? I picture myself from the other side of the street, a pale face in the corner of the glass. I'm being too obvious about it. Perhaps they're more practiced; they might have done this before, whatever *this* is.

Katie tugs on my sleeve, wanting me, her best auntie. I give a broad smile that feels pasted onto my face. It hurts my cheeks, but I smile and smile. JoJo is with her, so at least I can watch them together. Luke distracts Katie, wanting to show her a card trick. Her cry of delight pierces my brain like needles. I'm almost grateful for Luke then, though his presence is pulling my attention away from where it should be. *Now*, I keep thinking, and *now*, and *now*, but nothing happens.

The irritation hanging between Luke and Chloe warps the air. I don't know why he's stayed so long. Is he trying to show Chloe what a nice guy he is, playing with her little sister? Is he hoping she'll come around?

On the far side of the room, she and Shannon are having an argument. Shannon keeps laughing, is wearing a teasing expression. As I watch, she gives Chloe a little push towards Luke. I see the words on her lips: *You know you want to.*

But Chloe doesn't. She pushes Shannon back. Her expression closes up in fury and she crosses her slender arms across her chest. She must think she looks fierce, but to me she only looks very, very young and vulnerable, like someone could snap the bones of her wrists between their fingers. She tosses her long, gleaming hair over her shoulder, forcing Shannon to duck away. I want to watch them, too, every second, but I can't. I have to prioritise. JoJo first—then Chloe, then Shannon. That's what I saw, wasn't it? And Chloe will be screaming, but it will be too late by then, way too late…

Maybe I'm already too late.

Why didn't I get the two of them *out*?

Luke finishes his trick and Katie cheers. This is a distraction. I can't be distracted. Something is falling into place, I can feel it, something far more important than any petty crushes and annoyances. I look out of the window, more carefully this time, searching doorways and corners and bushes, looking for a broad-shouldered man with coldness in his eyes. I can't see him anywhere.

"Grace?" Leanne comes and stands next to me, taking advantage of a rare second of quiet. "You okay? I thought you might be ready for that glass of wine. This is a lot, I know."

I turn to her, relieved that it's just me and my friend for a second, and my resolution falters. A drink could help; it might banish my headache, steady my nerves. Then, then, I'll be able to think. "Why not?" I say. "Just one glass."

I follow her towards the kitchen.

Wine, yes. But also, I have an idea.

Leanne takes out two hefty glasses, pours generous measures. "Shouldn't, really," she grins. "But."

But. Right at this moment, I couldn't agree more. I raise my glass and we chink them together. It's chardonnay, syrupy and heavy, not really my taste, but I drink gratefully. Even with the lounge door open it's a hell of a lot quieter in here and I relish the lower volume, feel the slow, sweet warmth sink into me.

"I really appreciate you coming," Leanne says, patting me on the shoulder. "And the cake is awesome."

"Hidden talents," I joke, and raise my glass again. "I put some candles here somewhere. Silver balls and stuff. Why don't I get it ready now? One less thing to think about."

She agrees that it is, and leaves me to it.

First things first; I gulp back the wine, the level dropping as if it's lemonade. Then I strip the cling-film from the cake and shake six pink-and-white striped candles from their box. I press them into the chocolate one by one. It fragments into shards around the plastic holders and I'm tempted to put one on my tongue and allow it to melt, but I don't. Why should I get to taste it, when Katie isn't going to? That doesn't seem fair. It *isn't* fair, but it is for the best. For everyone.

I find the silver balls. There's no reason to bother, but somehow, I want this thing to be finished before it's done. I scatter some on top and they bounce and roll off. They never did go with chocolate, did they? Leanne would probably have known that, though she was too tactful to say. I hear the little pings as they hit the tiled floor and roll off into the corners. That doesn't matter, either. It's going to get so much worse.

I take the plate in my hands—my mother's plate, but that can't be helped, either. It feels as if things are happening as they should, as I've *seen*, as I hold it out in front of me and then let go.

The plate tilts as it falls. The cake slides, silver balls falling like rain, light little pings until the plate, that lovely, blue-flowered plate, shatters into pieces. The sponge is in clods. Like clumps of broken earth. There are crumbs everywhere, and sharp splinters of china, though the candles aren't lit, because I'm *changing* things, and then Leanne is there, *Oh Grace, what happened,* though she must think I have no grace, none at all, only that I'm clumsy, so very clumsy—

I hear a wail from Katie and Leanne whirls and guides her out of the door and shuts it in her face before she can see any more.

"I'm so sorry," I say. "I just slipped, that's all. There's so much on the table, I thought I could juggle, but—" my voice tails away. "So sorry. I hope Katie isn't too upset."

"Of course she is," Leanne snaps, her happy hosting demeanour slipping for a second. "She's already *seen* the mess. I only shut her out because of this." She waves a hand towards the sharp pieces of china that could cut little feet, that's all she sees of my mother's ruined plate, and for a second anger stirs inside me.

Leanne draws in a deep breath. "Look, it can't be helped, that's all. I'm sorry. Let me get this cleaned up."

The door opens again. It's not Katie, though; it's Chloe, come to see what's happened. "Oh my *God*," she says. "Poor Katie. It's her *birthday*."

I try to keep myself from smiling.

"You're right," I say. "Chloe, I'm really sorry, but why don't you and Shannon nip out in the car and pop to the shops? You could have a bit of time on your own, and maybe pick up a caterpillar cake. *Two* caterpillar cakes. I'll pay. It's just—I can't, I've had a drink, that's all." I indicate my wine glass, drained to the dregs. The honey sweetness of chardonnay is heavy in my mouth, weighting my tongue. "Giggles," I try to explain. "She'll like that, won't she? We need some of those."

She looks at me blankly, teenage contempt flashing in her eyes. She doesn't know what I'm talking about, and I feel like I've said enough, don't want to explain, but I pull my purse from my back pocket. She gives a slight shake of her head and goes to Leanne, who's already rummaging in her handbag. They murmur between them—*Could you, love? I know, sorry, love.* I tell myself I don't care, that it doesn't matter if my cake is spoiled or my friendships are bruised. I just want them to be safe, and they *will* be. This has worked out just right. Even Luke being here—the girls won't want to rush back with him around, will they? Chloe and Shannon will be away from here, the two of them out of harm's way, and I'll only have to worry about JoJo.

Then Chloe is gone. I hear her scooping up Shannon on her way through the lounge, and the front door opens and closes behind them. Leanne and I pick up clumps of sponge and shards of chocolate and fragments of broken plate and wipe up the mess and, for once, we hardly talk at all. When we're finished she still doesn't speak, just crosses the room and sticks her head around the door into the lounge.

"Who wants to play some games outside?" she says.

I hear a uniform cry of "*Me!*"

Leanne sets things up for pass the parcel, bringing out a CD player and a big package wrapped in newspaper. She's already strewn beanbags and cushions across the paving of the back yard. Luke, despite Chloe's absence, is still here. He must want to wait for her, hoping to see her again before he leaves. He helps the girls take their places and sits behind them to watch the game. Leanne crouches by the CD Player, her back to the group, so they can't accuse anyone of cheating. The music plays. Each girl clings to the precious parcel for a moment before passing it on. They scowl when

Ruby holds on a little too long, but the music doesn't stop and JoJo snatches it from her.

Leanne's yard is bounded by a high fence but, when I stand on tiptoe, I can just see over it into the alleyway that runs down the back. The asphalt is cracked and weeds are pushing through all over the place. I can't see anyone out there, unless they've ducked down against the wood. Is that what they're doing now, playing some party game of their own—hide and seek? I'm not tall enough to see, but it's so weird that he isn't here yet, that horrible man; a wrong note in the music. A sour taste among the sweet, sweet treats.

I realise this is my chance.

I step back into the kitchen and go through to the lounge, which is strewn with ripped wrapping paper and children's make-up and dolls and felt tips and soaps shaped like fruit and notepads and other gifts. I don't look out of the window. Instead, I open the front door—Chloe has left it on the latch so that anyone could walk in, silly Chloe—though for now, I leave it that way. I step out and reach for the balloon.

I take hold of the string more firmly this time, and wind it around the door handle, and then the balloon is in my hands. It tugs at me, wanting to be free. Wanting to fly. I release it and watch as it floats up, higher, into the air. *Happy Birthday!*

Now no one, no stranger passing by, would ever know there's a party going on in here for a bunch of innocent little girls.

The sweet thought threads through me, warm as wine, that maybe this is enough. Maybe I've changed things enough. Done the one simple thing that will save everything. Everyone.

Angels and ministers of grace defend us.

I look around once more before going back inside. There's a gap in the chain of parked cars where Leanne's Corsa had been. A little further along the road, a grey-haired old lady is walking towards me, dragging a shopping trolley with one hand, a reluctant Yorkshire terrier with the other. That's it; there's nothing else, no one in sight. I close the door behind me and release the Yale, making sure it's locked.

Visions of Grace

That done, I start to pick up the ripped wrapping paper and Katie's presents, making them tidy, putting everything straight. I hear occasional cheers and groans and fragments of music drifting from the back yard, though I'm glad to be alone for a while. At least I was right about the wine helping with my headache. It has, a little.

Then I slump onto the sofa, letting my hair hang in my face.

Outside, they've switched to some more exciting game. The girls are shrieking again. There's a brighter, clearer giggle as someone comes into the kitchen. Then Luke's voice, low and fiercely guttural. *Coming, ready or not!* Other sounds follow, shuffling and thudding, then a moment's quiet before there's a shriller cry and I realise I'm in the wrong place altogether.

Another cry. Not excitement; something else.

A scream.

Now.

I leap to my feet and run towards them.

What happens next comes in a burst of images. Everything is too sharp around the edges. Everything too bright.

There's a little girl lying on the ground in the yard. At first I think it's Katie, but of course it isn't; it's JoJo. Luke is standing over her. A pair of scissors is clutched in his hand. There's blood on the blades. The other girls are behind him, too scared, they should be running away but they're too shocked. I can tell they are because their mouths are open, all of them the same red, bright, bright red, but they aren't grinning any longer.

JoJo is red, too. There's red on her dress. On her legs, seeping into the ripped threads of those once-white patterned tights. Red smeared across her belly. More smeared across her cheek. Her hair, pulled loose, is straggled. Her eyes are too wide, but she isn't crying. This is beyond crying, beyond tears.

Now, I think.

No: not now.
Too late.

The thing I've been waiting for, watching for, was already here. It was already inside.

I feel a throb in my throat, beating in time with my heart. It feels like the air has swollen, pressing in, holding us in place.

Leanne is crouching next to JoJo, but she doesn't move. She's stricken, staring up at Luke. She's frozen. She's frozen because she wasn't expecting this. She isn't doing what a mum should do, what a mum needs to do, and I realise that's because it's me who needs to do that. It always has been.

But I'm too far away. Moment by moment, I see Luke raising the scissors and striking down. I see him slicing open her face, opening a new red grin. JoJo first. It always was, wasn't it?

She was always the one I needed to save.

Now. Now. Now…

What I'm envisioning with each second still doesn't happen. Luke hasn't gathered himself. He doesn't strike down again, not yet, though he still has hold of the scissors.

And I see everything. He thinks it's Katie he's stabbed. She and JoJo look so very much alike, and Luke doesn't know her all that well because it's never been Katie he's interested in. That's Chloe, she's who he wants, but he can't have her and he hates her for that, for not wanting him back, for being so very beautiful and so very out of reach. He hates her for scorning him, for leaving him here at her house all alone. He's feeling hurt and humiliated and here is the result. Chloe's not even in the house—I got her out of the way—so he's lashed out at what he could reach: a little girl, the one he thinks Chloe loves most in this world. That's it, it was Chloe's heart he was striking at, what he imagines he's sliced open and left lying on the floor, only it wasn't Chloe's little sister, after all. It was her very best friend, JoJoJoJoJo…

Luke stands with his head lowered, his hair not quite covering the cold, bright shine in his eyes. And at last, I recognise them.

Visions of Grace

It's *him*.

It was always him.

I'd always been seeing into the future. I'd been having *visions*. With Luke, I'd just seen a little further forward, that's all. I'd been seeing him *after*. Not like this, a young lad, just starting out; no, my mind had known that something was going to happen, and instead I'd seen the dark-eyed, louring, unkempt man who would be the result of it. I'd been seeing what Luke will look like at forty or fifty, when the import of this day has sunk into him. When his guilt and his shame have rotted his bones from the inside; when he's spent more than half his life in prison.

But it's already too late. It must be, because he's letting go of the scissors. He's letting them fall into Leanne's open hand.

They're safe, I think. *The other girls are safe. But JoJo isn't, not yet.*

JoJo's eyes are fixed and wide. She's conscious, but for how long? It was always JoJo I had to protect. Like a guardian; like a *mum*. I rush forward and scoop her into my arms. The spell breaks, and the other girls cry out and shrink away, as if it's only now that they can move. Clasping her close—she's so light in my arms—I hurry for the door. Leanne calls after me and for a moment I think it's a warning, that Luke is coming after me, and the skin on my back crawls, waiting for a hand to grab me, but it doesn't happen. I keep moving. I release the lock on the front door with one hand and I am outside.

"You're safe, JoJo," I keep saying. "I'll get you to a hospital. It'll be fine. It'll all be fine, now."

I hurry to my own car. Determination is welling inside me again, giving me the strength I need to hold her, balancing her little body in my arms as I retrieve my keys from my pocket and press the button to unlock the doors.

JoJo cries out as I manoeuvre her into the back. "Sorry JoJo, I'm sorry it hurts, I know." I lay her across the seats—I should sit her up, fasten a seatbelt around her, but this is hardly the time to worry about rules, and wouldn't being upright make her bleed more? At least she's still conscious, there's that. I grab her hand for a moment, squeezing her fingers to let her know I'm with her, then I run around to the driver's side.

As I pull away from the kerb, I catch a glimpse of Leanne's pale, shocked face in her doorway, staring after me. *Look after the others,* I think, *Don't let him do anything else, don't let things change, not now.* I send up a silent prayer that Luke is still slumped in place, all the strength gone out of him. That he'll stay that way until the police arrive, that he won't snatch the scissors again or a knife, that he won't attack Katie or Daisy or Isla or Ruby or Em.

But he *can't*. I'd have *seen* it, wouldn't I?

Now my visions are a comfort as I stamp on the accelerator, all the parked cars becoming a blur at my side. From the corner of my eye I see the old lady with her shopping trolley and terrier, further down the road and still sauntering, pausing to stare at whoever's driving so fast.

JoJo, behind me, wails.

Hold on, baby. I've saved Chloe and Shannon. I've done that much. Why not JoJo, too? Otherwise, what was the point?

I have to save JoJo, too.

I push the car faster. I tell myself that JoJo's crying can only be a good thing. Silence would be worse. The kind of silent she'd been when I saw her sitting on my sofa. Staring through her straggling, draggly hair...

Thank all the gods, she must be feeling a little stronger. Her voice is closer to me when she speaks, as if she's trying to sit up. She's still confused, though. "I fell", she says. "I fell."

"I know. Lie down, sweetness," I say. "Then you won't fall again."

I hear a sniffle. "I want my mummy."

"*I'm* here, JoJo," I say. "*I'm* helping you." At first that's how I say the words, with the emphasis on the *I*—*I'm* here, *not your mum*, but after that I don't bother.

"I want my mummy," she says.

"I'm here, JoJo," I answer. "I'm helping you."

And I am. The distinction doesn't matter, not now. We're together, and she's safe. That's what matters. To a mum, that's all that ever matters.

We're almost at the end of the road. On the opposite side from all the parked cars, a man is emerging from a gate, a crumpled orange plastic bag held in one hand. His head twists towards us, gawking as the old lady had. I don't care. The determination inside has taken hold of me, taken me over. The corner is coming up fast but I'm not going to slow, not yet, and I grip the wheel tighter, just as a car turns into the road in front of me.

It's red. It's bright red, a red *Corsa*, and I know the road isn't wide enough, and I'm going too fast, and I already know that I can't stop even as I slam on the brakes, yet everything seems to happen so, so slowly. My gaze shifts from the outline of the red car to the person in the driver's seat. Chloe is looking back at me. As I watch, her mouth falls open. Shannon is beside her, staring in shock, and her mouth is open too but only a little. She's frozen. Chloe, though; Chloe is screaming. And there isn't time, not for anything. I yank on the wheel and the car's tyre hits the kerb and then the whole world judders. Everything is in motion.

I sense, rather than see, a shape fly past me. I feel its physicality; I feel how movement lends it weight as it collides with the glass. I hear the sound it makes.

JoJo, I'm saying, or perhaps it's *no, no. JoJo, no. Nonononono...*

The world judders again. I hear smashing and crushing and splintering. A broken plate, but so much *more*. And still everything is moving.

There is a single moment of clarity. It can be no more than that; a second in time, but it seems to stretch out forever. The man has stepped out of his gate. He's turning towards the road. He is broad and stocky. His posture is stooped, his head hunched into his shoulders, and his shirt is an unwashed shade of white. His hair is unkempt and his chin is unshaven and he isn't wearing any expression at all but his eyes narrow into a glare, turning colder and harder as two cars, smashed into a single entity, bear down on him.

Then he doesn't look angry any longer.

He only looks afraid.

CHAPTER SEVEN
After the Party

The world is upside down. Nothing is as it should be. My headache is redoubled and everything throbs and burns, like smouldering candles. I blink and blink, but nothing resolves. My forehead feels wet, like I've been sweating, but I don't feel hot. I'm cold, all over. There is something next to me in the car; on the *ceiling* of the car, which is beneath me now, instead of over my head.

I don't want to look at it, but I must. When I twist my neck, my whole spine lights up and I let out a gasp. The sound is wordless, but I hear words anyway, or one word. No: a name.

JoJoJoJoJo...

I force my hands to move across the space between us. I try to scoop her into my arms like I did in Leanne's back yard, but I can't. I can't hold her. I can't be her mum. All I manage to do is grasp one thin little arm, so very small under my hands. When I try to pull her towards me she feels so loose; her whole body shifts and rolls. I try instead to take hold of her dress, her pretty, pink, flared party dress. *Mine*, I think. *She's mine.* I know that isn't true, not really, but in this moment, it is; she's mine, my little girl.

I look at her again and see something impossible.

I try to focus. To take her all in.

Red on her lips. The red smear on her cheek. It isn't blood; it's make-up. They were playing at make-up, weren't they? All of them, sitting in a ring.

The smear on her dress. It bears the imprint of fingers. The shape of a hand. Not his, that bastard's; it's too small for that. It's *her* handprint. She must have put her hand to the wound when he cut her, then put her hand to her waist. Maybe she wanted to wipe the blood off. The fabric of her dress is stained, but not sliced open or torn. There's no wound, not there. That's good, isn't it?

Her leg. That's where he hurt her; that's where most of the blood is. I can see that clearly, but also something else; something that shouldn't be there.

There's a shard of broken china jutting from the wound.

For a second I focus on JoJo's blank, blank eyes. I blink and the world around me, treacherous, swims. Then it comes into focus once more, too sharp, sharp enough to cut. Blurs once more. *Blink.* In and out. It doesn't matter if I can see it clearly; I recognise that china. I'd know it anywhere. I should. It still has a little scrap of a blue flower on its edge, just visible through JoJo's blood.

It's a part of my mother's plate. The one I'd used to carry Katie's birthday cake.

I recognise it. But I don't know how it came to be here.

Now, I think. But that isn't what I mean.

Then. That is what I need to see.

I'd been fiddling with the front door. Messing with that balloon, checking the street, when I should have been worrying about who was already inside. I'd been tidying the lounge, for God's sake—not with the girls, where I should have been. But I'd been listening to them, hadn't I? I'd heard them plainly enough. Squealing, playing some game, and then one of them had run into the kitchen.

The kitchen where my mother's plate had shattered into a hundred pieces.

Leanne and I had cleaned it up, but she'd been stressed, hadn't she? In a hurry. And me—I'd been reeling from the wine. I'd been thinking about what was going to happen, not what was happening *then*. I had been distracted. Both of us were. Had we picked up every single piece? Or had we missed one?

I see again the way that Leanne had ushered Katie out of the kitchen, closing the door in her face, so that she wouldn't cut her feet...

But later, during that game, one of the girls had run inside. I'd heard that. I'd heard Luke run after her. That fierce, guttural voice. *Coming, ready or not!*

Playing a game.

Just playing a game.

Something else comes back to me then, from what seems like a long time ago, from another world. Katie's voice. *I want to play tig!*

Katie had said that, hadn't she, and she was the birthday girl, and birthday girls always get what they want, don't they?

I fell, JoJo had said. *I fell. I fell...*

Luke had chased her into the kitchen. She'd been excited, going too fast. I see it now as if it's in front of me: JoJo looking over her shoulder, shrieking at the *monster* running after her, her feet slipping on the floor, which was imperfectly wiped, possibly still damp, and there, waiting for her, was that shard of ceramic. Pointed. Sharp. Ready to bury itself in her soft skin.

I close my eyes. What had I heard? A shuffling. A thud. Shrieks, turning into a scream.

And what had Luke done then? What *would* he do?

I try to picture him, still a monster, still in chase, enraged by the sight of blood, wanting more. Snatching up the scissors, opening the blades, raising them over his head.

But the picture dissolves in front of me. I try to hold onto it, *needing* it, but I can't see it any longer.

Instead, I see Luke helping JoJo to her feet. Seeing the blood, picking her up, carrying her outside. Because that's where Leanne is, isn't it? And Leanne is a mum. Mums always know what to do.

Visions of Grace

That's when the other girls had screamed. They'd seen the blood, the broken skin. They'd seen JoJo's patterned tights all torn and fraying, ruined, the whiteness of them turning to red, that ugly splinter of china jutting out.

No. Not just torn.

Because I see that now, too. JoJo's tights are shredded, but in the middle of the loose threads is a straight line, carved straight across the pattern. Because it wouldn't have been any use trying to take off those tights around that piece of china, would it? No, they would have needed to be cut away. They'd have to be cut off with scissors before the shard could be removed and everything cleaned up. They'd got blood on the scissors when they did it, I'd seen that, Luke had been holding them up in his hand, they'd have needed to clean those, too…

I close my eyes. I feel sick. My pain feels like it's a long way away. I see Luke's face. His eyes are cold and hard, but not with rage; only at the sight of JoJo's leg, the fearsomeness of blood, their simple, happy game suddenly turned to *this*. But he'd tried to do what was best. He had taken her to Leanne, who probably already had those scissors ready, because they were playing pass the parcel, weren't they? That big newspaper bundle was made of layers and layers of paper, all taped together. It would have got smaller and smaller, until the last layer was more Sellotape than wrap, so difficult for little fingers to open.

No. He stabbed JoJo. He was a monster. I saved her…

I shift my gaze from JoJo's blank eyes to another flash of red, this one worse than any other. A single wound, high in the centre of JoJo's pale, smooth forehead. I stare and stare, but no matter how I do, this one doesn't change.

It is real, real, real.

I drift. And I find myself trying to remember something else: that one last cry as I'd rushed out of the house with JoJo clutched in my arms. I hear it over and over, but no matter how I try, I can't make out the words. I can hear the intonation, though, and it isn't how I'd thought it was. Or is it becoming distorted in my memory? I no longer know, but it seems to me now there might have been a question in it. *Where are you going?* perhaps. Or maybe, *What are you doing?*

It plays over and over in my mind. Each moment, standing out clear among other moments. Any one of them in which I could have done something else, anything else. *Changed* things. But they keep on happening in the same way, again and again and again. Moving forward in time, winding back. *Now*. And *now*. And *now*.

A little further away, beyond the things crowding my mind, is a red car. The door and side panel are hopelessly crumpled, the windscreen so smashed it's all but opaque. I'm grateful for that, but I can see inside it anyway. I can see Chloe. She's always screaming, now. I can see Shannon too, her face white with horror, seeing the thing that is coming for her, but not screaming; not able to scream.

And the stranger. The man. He came next. Of course he did. That's how I'd seen them, wasn't it? Right from the beginning. First JoJo, dead before the cars had even finished moving. Chloe next. Then Shannon, her friend, and him last of all, looking at me like that, staring, *glaring*—

I can't see him now, though. I don't know where he is. Pasted against a wall? Crushed under one of the cars? I'm glad I don't know.

I allow my gaze to turn upward, through my own windscreen, marred by one splintering crack, beads of blood clinging to it, along with a few strands of hair. I look past them, through them, wondering if I'll see a pink balloon floating up against the grey sky, *Happy Birthday!*, but I don't. My car has come to a rest facing a wall, and the darkness of the brick has turned the glass into an imperfect mirror. I see only the faint outline of a woman's face, looking down on me. And I drift. Like my vision, like the whole world around me, I drift.

Chapter Eight
When I was Five

I stare up at the form hovering above me. Just like then. Like I'm back at the beginning, in my very first memory. I'm looking up into the half-dark, staring at the shape leaning over me, and it is indistinct, impossible to make out the features, like nothing more than a reflection in darkened, broken glass. I can't properly make out her face. It's hazy, wavering around the edges, then she tilts her head and everything clarifies and I see into her eyes.

My mother still doesn't speak. She only looks. There is something not quite right about her face. She's too pale. There's something wrong with the way she's looking at me. It's as if she's seeing everything: my future, or perhaps hers. All that I have inside, everything I *am*. She sees those things and still she doesn't smile.

I keep hearing a sound. Something pressing in at the edges of my consciousness, though I'm not sure it's really there. Still, I know it's important. An engine growling. Screeching. Glass smashing. Metal crumpling. Not here, but a very long, long way away.

Mum doesn't seem to hear it. She's come to tuck me in, or I thought she had, but she doesn't move, and she still doesn't say anything. She just goes on looking, and eventually, quietly, I start to cry.

I feel the tears, warm on my face, and something inside me unlocks. I see what I had forgotten, the place I never wanted to go, the thing that Dad never told me. I see what happened next; I see the end of the story.

I rub at my eyes. I can still feel the force of my mother's stare, but when I open them, my room is empty. For a second I'm too surprised to cry any longer. I hadn't heard her move. Hadn't even sensed it. She didn't say goodnight after all. I hadn't heard the scrape of the door over the carpet; she must have slipped out through the gap and left it open behind her. I'm not sure how she managed that. The door's only slightly ajar, barely enough light entering the room to make out my wardrobe, my chest of drawers, my big old teddy bear sitting at my desk. All my familiar, expected things—except for *her*.

An unwelcome, shadowy, whispery part of my mind wakes, and it shows me an image of my mum, too slender, slithery, sliding to the floor and under my bed like a monster in a fairy tale. I shake my head: *No*. Mum wouldn't play tricks on me, not that kind anyway; not the mean, cruel kind. She's my *mum*, and anyway, it feels like my room is empty.

My heartbeat making itself felt, something insistent knocking inside my chest, I push my cuddly bunny away, get out of bed and cross the floor. My bare feet don't make much of a sound, but when I open the door it does, *shushing* across the carpet just as it always has. I pad down the stairs, and as I go the burbling of the television reaches my ears; urgent voices that aren't really here, some boring, grown-up programme Mum and Dad are watching.

I hear Dad's voice, a sleepy murmur. "Want me to go, love?"

And I hear Mum's reply. "That's all right, I'll tuck her in. Just one—more—minute. In the adverts."

I sit down on the stairs, still listening. Frowning. I don't understand. Mum already came up. Has she forgotten—like she forgot to tuck me in, as she always does?

I replay the last few minutes. Mum's face leaning over me, so clear in my mind. She came in, she did, but I never heard her go out again and now she's here, with Dad, so drowsy I can picture her snuggled against him on the sofa, her head on his chest, her feet tucked under the cushions. Watching something on telly. So absorbed she doesn't want to move, not quite yet. Not till the adverts are on.

I feel cold right through. I think of walking into the lounge and looking at her for real, even picture myself doing it, but somehow I can't. I don't *want* to see her. I can't stay here though, because I don't want her to come out and see me. Is it really my mum in there—or something else?

Was that not Mum, leaning over my bed?

It had looked so very like her. I could have reached out and touched her skin.

A thought strikes me, and I push myself up enough to turn and peer back up the stairs, where my door remains open. The others on the landing are closed. I picture Mum, or a paler, quieter version of her, leaning against one of those doors now and listening for me. Is that where she is? Can she hear my breathing—my heartbeat?

I want my mum to come and wrap her arms around me. To feel her hair brushing my face. But where is she?

I can't go back up the stairs. I can't go into the lounge.

I can't move.

I blink. All there is in front of me is our front door.

That's when I think of Mia, my very best friend. She lives across the road, in the house straight opposite. She has a dog called Cookie, with a wet, sniffy nose and a waggy tail and her mum and dad are cheerful and happy and loud. *Normal.* I don't know why that word should seem important—we're normal, too, aren't we?—and then I hear stirring in the lounge, the TV gets louder with some cheery, jangly tune, and I think I know.

I hurry to the door, reach up and undo the latch, then quietly pull the door towards me. The letterbox rattles, just a little—it always does, I should have thought of it, but it's too late now. I stare for a split-second at the sight of the nubbly concrete path, at my own bare feet, then I tell myself to be brave like a princess in a story and I step out all at once. I'm halfway to the gate before I know it. Mia's house isn't far. It's not like this is difficult. I've been over there—*with Mum, my real, actual Mum*—hundreds of times.

But not in the dark. Not in the cold. Not without anyone knowing where I'm going.

I let the door close behind me. This time the lock rattles as it falls into place. For some reason I think of a party game: hide and seek.

Coming, ready or not!

And she is. Suddenly I know she is, she's hurrying to that same door, Mum, or someone who looks just like her, but *not* her—

I run.

There is a burst of images, everything too sharp around the edges, everything a little too bright. The peeling gate, rough under my hands. It slams as the spring snaps it closed behind me. Streetlights reveal circles of cracked asphalt in the road. And there, surely smaller than it should be, too small, is Mia's front door, familiar, red, lit by a lantern set over the frame.

A letterbox rattles. There's a shout—a familiar voice, or is it something else—one that only sounds that way?

I run harder. And there are other lights, brighter than before, brighter than anything, growing bigger, and noise—

An engine growling. Screeching.

Mum's voice, but not like Mum's voice at all.

There is smashing glass and crumpling metal.

The second memory I possess from when I was five-and-a-half, though I had forgotten it for so long, is also of my mother's face. It is like the first, the one I had held so dear, but this time the image is inverted.

I am leaning over her. She is lying on the ground. Her hair is everywhere, strewn across the tarmac. She'd hate that, getting it dirty. And her face is so familiar, even though there is something wrong with it. She's so very pale. Too pale.

I hear voices, but they seem to be coming from a long way away.

Mum doesn't say anything, though I wait. She just stares up at me, and it is as if she sees everything: all that I have inside. Everything I *am*. She sees all of those things and yet she still doesn't smile. She just goes on staring, until the moment when she stops seeing those things and starts seeing nothing at all.

Later, I will forget. I will cling to another memory, a better one. Mum tucking me in, like she always did. The lines of her face. The colour of her eyes. My first and best memory of my mother. Or at least, the closest thing I have. In truth, I cannot be certain if it was her; whether it was something that really happened, or only an image in my head. Whether that sight of her face, so very vivid, so very complete, was ever real at all.

Now I stare up at the face looking down at me, reflected in the cracked glass of a broken windscreen. Yet strangely, the words that come to me are my father's. A conversation we would not have until years later.

Grace, I was saying. *Grace. You mean like in church?*

Well, I don't rightly know, love, he'd replied. *We never really went to church, did we?*

And I remember: I had tried so hard to say the words that were in my mind, the ones that came next, or that should have come next.

What am I, then?

Grace, but never graceful. *Grace*, but not the kind from church; not an angel. Something bestowed, though; oh yes, I was that. But what? *Grace… Grace… Grace.*

I had wanted, so very much, to be all of the things that word could possibly mean. Beautiful, wonderful, magical things.

I force my lips to whisper those words now.

What am I, then?

And I wait. But the answer doesn't come.

Acknowledgements

Thanks firstly to Marie O'Regan, since this novella wouldn't exist if you hadn't asked me to write it! Thanks too to Pete and Nicky Crowther, Mike and Sheryl Smith, and the whole lovely team at PS Publishing. And I was blown away by Beatriz Martin Vidal's beautiful artwork—thank you, Beatriz!

A big shout goes out to early readers, Gary McMahon and Daniel Church. I'm also grateful to the indie presses, editors, bloggers and other enthusiasts who inject life into the world of short stories and novellas. And of course my thanks go to you, the reader.

Last but never least, thanks too to my partner, Fergus.